DARKNESS EXPOSED

Cyprus Hart

PRAISE FOR DARKNESS WITHIN

"In Darkness Within, *Hart spins fantasy creature lore in delightfully unexpected directions, then builds a suspenseful journey where main characters, Drew and Aideen, are as unsure about each other as they are about making it out alive. Add in plenty of will-they-won't-they steam and I'm impatient for more!"* - Poppy Minnix, Author

"If you like Nalini Singh and Ilona Andrews, you'll love Darkness Within, *a fantastic new novel from Cyprus Hart. Aideen and Druain are scorching hot together and take enemies-to-lovers to a whole new level."* - Bestselling author Raisa Greywood

"That was intense and funny all at once". - J.L. Bowman, Author of *The Weekend*

www.BOROUGHSPUBLISHINGGROUP.com

DARKNESS EXPOSED
Copyright © 2021 Cyprus Hart

ISBN: 978-1-953810-77-9

DARKNESS EXPOSED

CHAPTER ONE

Aideen

The smooth glide of wheels over the pavement would be comforting if it wasn't for the large and dangerous dwarf sitting in the driver's seat.

Druain Lindberg, criminal, killer, and seven feet of muscle and beard.

I can't believe it's only been an hour since Drew's iron control snapped and he took me rough, intense, and unrestrained. I'm not complaining, although I expect I'll be sore the longer I sit in this vehicle. Right before we got horizontal, he'd killed a dragon and four people, all in the "safety" of his secret cabin.

He'd gotten me to the cabin as part of his plan to keep me protected from my—now our—enemies. But his boss, a vampire underworld crime boss, Stefen Costecu, had found us, and sent minions to kill us.

We're fleeing to who knows where with no plan and no idea if anyone is chasing us. As I stare out my window, the forest flashes by on either side of this one lane highway. I should be afraid or at least worried, but all I feel is determination and a tinge of excitement. This is the most impulsive and dangerous thing I've ever done, and the high and full-on rush of sex and violence hasn't worn off yet. I keep expecting to come to my senses, snap out of it, demand to be taken back home so I can sort out everything, but the minutes tick by and I say nothing.

"What are you thinking, Zero?" Lindberg's low rumble breaks into my musing.

Miss Duffy might be a bit formal after all we've done with our bodies, but is it too much to ask he at least call me Aideen? He seems determined to stick with the nickname he came up with after he kidnapped me from the secret prison where I'd locked him up. It's hard to believe it's been an hour since our adult activities, but it's even more unbelievable it's only been a few days since he upended my life.

What a simple time it'd been before then. I was content with my job of protecting humans from rogue creatures like Drew and his boss. With the help of the organization I'm part of, we investigate and lock up all sorts of criminals from werewolves to vampires to ghouls. All that's changed.

Even something as simple as a bath seems different. As a selkie, baths are more than places to relax and get clean. My stare is drawn to my fingers, which show no sign of the breaks suffered when Drew was forced to snap them. After taking shower in his cabin, I completely repaired. For selkies, water is the fountain of youth.

He's apologized, and it was necessary at the time, so I can't be too upset. He's more than made up for it with the multiple times he's saved my life since then.

So here I am being driven by the man who broke my fingers and pulled out my toenail, all because he's really a hero of sorts, and he ignites this flame in my stomach, which spreads to other parts of my body like wildfire. He's pretty good at the whole sex thing, and he made sure I was taken care of first.

"Zero?" he asks again.

"What? Oh. Nothing."

"I don't believe that," he says. He reaches out, grabs a lock of my hair, trails his fingers down as it drapes over my shoulder, and then gives it a tug.

"Ow, you jerk." I grab at the sting in my head and turn to scowl to cover my secret and worrying desire to have him pull it harder. I never wanted to get a tattoo because I was scared of the pain, yet around him everything is flipped. I shove down the memory of those three hard spanks he'd given my ass. "What are you, five?"

"You know you like it." His grin is infuriating.

"Shut up. No, I don't."

His reply is cut off by a curse as a deer gallops across the road in front of us, sunlight dappling across its hide. My heart leaps as the SUV swerves to avoid hitting the animal. I almost bang my head on the window from the sudden movement. He stops on the shoulder.

"You okay?"

"Yeah. Startled."

"Sorry. My driving skills aren't what they used to be."

"Driving skills? You mean besides pushing the pedals and moving the steering wheel?"

He ignores my barb and stares intensely, which I'm learning means he's thinking about something. "You know I'm the one who's been feeding you information from the inside, right?"

"Yep. I figured that out. Somewhere around the second corpse."

He grunts noncommittally and pulls back onto the road. "Did you ever meet my handler?"

Glancing at him out of the corner of my eye, I'm trying to decide where this line of questioning is going. I shrug. "No. Whoever it was reported to higher-ups, and they filtered the information down. For security reasons. Why?"

"Curious." His fingers beat an arrhythmic staccato on the fake leather steering wheel. "You know, she—"

Whatever he was going to say is interrupted by a massive crash, shattering glass, crunching metal, a jumble of sharp and discordant sounds. It's so sudden for several suspended moments, I don't notice we're tumbling through the air, rolling over and over, flinging me in every direction possible within the confines of my seatbelt.

As sudden as the crash starts it ends with a final creak and groan of metal. Through my window is the sky, through Drew's window is pavement. My seatbelt holds me in place, dangling to the side, cutting into my hip and neck. The airbags are flaccid, having given their lives to keep us from bashing in our brains against the dashboard.

There're too many wrong things to notice at once. Steam from the wrecked engine in front of us, pain in my knee, head, and arm. Drew is grimacing, has a cut across his forehead, and his hands still grip the wheel.

"Fuck. Get out, Zero," he croaks.

"You're bleeding."

"Get out. Now." Something in his tone brooks no argument, a tone he's used only a couple times before, and always for a reason. I grab at my buckle, manage to click it open, and tumble to land on him.

"Sorry," I say, trying to get my feet under me on the center console without stepping on him so I can open my door and get out.

"Oof."

I fling open the door only for it to crash to the ground. I pull myself up, wiggling across the battered metal of the passenger side of the SUV and drop to the ground. Standing makes me a little dizzy, as if seeing the SUV on its side is somehow tilting my world. I rub my forehead to try to clear the lingering confusion of the accident, ignoring the aches. There's water in the vehicle, I can use that to heal whatever minor injuries I might have.

I notice the other car at the same time Lindberg starts yelling again. Of course, there had to be another car. What else would we have hit? Before I can run over and make sure the people are okay, the words being shouted pierce the fog enveloping my brain.

"Zero. Get away," His voice becomes clearer on the last shout as his head emerges from the passenger side opening.

His warning gives me a split-second to assess the situation, surveying everything as I'm trained to do. The accident shook me up, but some semblance of observational skill limps back.

The SUV we were in is on the side, but from where I'm standing, I can see the huge dent in the rear driver's side quadrant. It's right where it should be to spin out a car. The other vehicle is a black SUV similar to ours. The damage on the front end was absorbed by the massive grill, hanging off and dented.

There are no skid marks on the pavement from where the crash happened.

Movement in the other SUV catches my eye. Four people, shaking off the impact. No panicked looks, no open mouths of shock or apology. Large people. Super large people.

"Zero," Lindberg shouts again.

The eyes on the emerging non-human from the other SUV give him away. He tosses his shattered sunglasses aside. The pupils aren't round as they should be. They're slits, like you'd expect from a reptile. I'm already backing up, but the man strikes with surprising speed. If his naga heritage wasn't obvious before, it is now.

My brain can't stop over-thinking, even as I'm tossed aside like a ragdoll before his fist can hit me. It whistles over my head, and he hits Drew right in the middle of his chest. A solid crunching sound matches my feet scrabbling on the gravel on the side of the road.

Mere hours ago, he took on three assailants by himself, but he caught those attackers off guard. No one's going to be nice enough to be caught off guard now. To make matters worse, a second SUV screeches up and the doors fly open, disgorging more attackers.

"Now would be an excellent time to listen to me, for once, and run," he shouts the last word while breaking the arm of the naga, which is a nice feat considering how flexible they are.

I count six more people, vampires, werewolves, and a ghoul. "I can help," I protest, while everything in me is screaming for me to get out of there. The sex wasn't that great. Okay. That's a lie.

"Help by escaping and then rescuing me if I'm still alive," he grunts. It's a miracle he can get all those words out, what with being jumped by three people at once.

I'm about to protest again, and I almost take a step forward, but then the last door on the trailing SUV opens. I can sense who it is before he appears around the dark glass. Costecu.

"Hello, my dear," he says. His voice isn't raised, but it still carries across the scuffle happening between us. His smile is polite and laced with menace.

"For fuck's sake, Zero," Drew shouts, surging forward to put himself between us, dragging resisting antagonists with him. I'm already turning to run. I'm not stupid brave. I know a lost fight when I see one.

I'm wearing Drew's spare set of clothes, my own casualties of blood and mud, torn beyond salvation during my ordeal. If he were a normal man, his clothes might almost fit me, since I top out at almost six feet, but he's a foot taller and has over a hundred and fifty pounds of muscle padding his magnificent body. I'm swimming in his slacks and button-up shirt. No amount of rolling the sleeves or cuffs help.

The socks I'm glad I insisted on wearing are the only protection against sticks and rocks as I scramble down the embankment, listening for any signs of pursuit as I head deeper into the woods. They're bound to chase after me, but maybe Drew can delay them for a few minutes.

Rescue. He wants me to rescue him. I have no idea how I'm going to pull that off, but he's right. I will come back for him. No one's going to take him away from me just when we were getting to the exciting parts. The shouting fades away.

A snap of twigs alerts me. I have at least one pursuer. It's tempting to turn around to check, but I'd end up tripping over something, and wouldn't gain any knowledge I don't already have. I need to focus on getting away.

Concentrating on going forward, not worrying about direction yet since the only one that matters is away, I draw on memories of my track and field days in college. I was too tall to ever be better than average, but the strategies for long distance running come to mind.

Steady breathing, find your pace, don't push too hard. If they haven't caught up to you in the first couple hundred meters, and you don't exhaust yourself, it becomes a matter of endurance. Stay ahead and hope they run out of steam first.

Like I said, I was average at best, but I *was* on the team. As long as it's not a werewolf, who could lope forever and a day, I should be okay. Shit, it's probably a werewolf. It'd be the smart thing to do.

Trying to keep myself calm, dodging trees that hinder the whole "find your stride" thing, I go over my options. If it's a vampire, they'll give up the quickest. They like stalking, but not chasing more than a mile or two. They're the cheetahs. Fast bursts, then they burn out. Ghouls can go for quite a while, but they're not fast at all. They're like warthogs, all ugly and snorty, but they'd rather pick on easy victims.

There's no way it's Costecu coming after me. He would've run me down minutes ago unless he's playing with me. Nah. He wouldn't leave Drew with the henchmen. It doesn't seem like something Costecu would trust them to do by themselves. I can see him gloating in that old world politeness he has. Telling Drew how he's going to capture me too, then torture us both over several days or weeks.

That's assuming Drew doesn't come out the victor, which is something I'd like to pretend would happen, but seven against one are incredible odds. He's not Superman.

My lungs are burning. This is way more exercise than I do in the gym, and I haven't done any jogging in a long time. I've been too busy at my job, tracking down Costecu and Drew. There's no time for trivial matters like personal health when there's so much danger out in the world.

Over my breath cycling in and out, and my sore feet making faint sounds in the leaves, I listen for signs of pursuit. Is that a rock being kicked? A bush being shoved aside? I can't tell. I have no choice but to keep going and hope I've gotten away.

After another thirty minutes of not slowing down, I've reached my limit. I've pushed myself too hard, not quite able to dampen the fear of getting caught. I have to stop.

A fallen log off to my left catches my attention, promising shelter, however temporary. It looks like bush and dirt have built up around it, creating a small and dirty hollow underneath where I can duck in.

One final mental finger cross and I veer over to it and throw myself down. Clawing at leaves to cover myself up as much as possible, not that it would help much, I slow my breathing and wait.

The only sounds are the ambient noises of nature, slow to come back after being disturbed by a noisy and clumsy selkie dashing through their home. I don't move.

Five minutes pass, then ten, then fifteen, no one shows up. Did I get away? I must have. I don't care how, and I don't care why, but no one is here to drag me away.

Now for step two.

Figuring out where the heck I am, getting back to civilization, and rescuing Drew.

Easy.

CHAPTER TWO

Druain

It took too long, but Zero runs off, the crunch of her socked feet across gravel a huge relief. No matter what happens, as long as she gets away, it'll all work out. Now I need to do my job of distracting them and keeping as many here as I can.

Shouting and swinging my fists, I attempted to find the werewolves and stop them from going anywhere. They're the last thing I want running off after Zero. While I have grown some confidence in her strength of survival, there's no reason to risk it. I need to give her every advantage I can.

Dragging people after me, I slog through the melee, making my way toward Costecu. If I can threaten him, they'll all stay to protect their leader.

"Go get her," he spits out, eyes boring against my own angry gaze. Someone moves to run, and I lunge sideways to grab at their legs. The sudden movement takes everyone with me, and I find my target, yanking them to the pavement. A nasty crack sounds my success in stopping the one attacker, but the downside is I'm on the ground.

Bodies hit me, piling on top, forcing me down as I try to push back up. Straining, willing my muscles to work even if they never work again, I manage to rise to one knee before the blows start to break past my dwarven toughness. I can't ignore damage and pain forever.

I've got to hold out as long as possible. Keep them busy until I can't anymore. The random flash of an image, the thought of Costecu capturing Zero again gives me another shock to my system, enough for me to surge upright and throw off two of my attackers.

Punches flash left and right. Hitting is my goal, what or how doesn't matter.

Something breaks my ribs, right in the spot where that damn golem had nailed me all those days ago. Focus. Costecu is about ten feet away and I make getting to him my goal, a target to work toward. He's staring me down, and I no longer break eye contact. I force my feet to move, though they feel heavy and slow.

Pain blooms, wavers, and dulls. Everything is tense and taut, like my bones have rusted together. My joints creak with the strain of moving forward. What must be hands grab at me, feet kick, trying to trip me. I reach out with a free hand, noting the blood smeared over my skin, not knowing if it's mine, and I don't care. A couple more inches and I can grab him.

The world tilts and spins, and the highway rushes up to smack me in the side of the head. Stars burst against my eyes, blinding me with a cornucopia of sparkles. Thumps pound in my ears, blotting out any sort of sound. I smell iron.

I'm still breathing, and I'm not willing to give up. I swing with my legs, connecting with something on someone at the same time as I'm grabbed by the head. Asphalt is a lot harder than fists. The blacktop crashes against my face time and again.

The flashing colors start to go dim. I can take a lot of abuse, but everyone has their limit. I don't want to be unconscious for any period of time. It might be time to pretend like I'm giving up, let them take me, and save myself for whatever's next.

I try to say "stop," but only a ragged groan escapes my throat. My mouth seems to be swollen shut. I groan louder.

"Hold."

That must be Costecu, although he sounds like he's underwater, or maybe I'm underwater. No one else would dare say anything.

"Are you trying to say something, Mr. Lindberg?"

He's closer, perhaps right next to my ear. Maybe they've stopped hitting me, but it's hard to tell. Breathing is hard, as if the air isn't going into my lungs, but instead somewhere else. My vision resolves and I can see distinct blobs instead of one big blob. The blobs are standing over me, waiting.

"Hnng."

"I'm sorry, I couldn't hear that." Costecu sounds sincere, which means he's feeling superior and in control. I'll let him continue to believe that. I could break his neck if I wanted, I'm sure. Okay, so my arms won't move, but I need only a few minutes to get my juice back. He can be smug all he wants. I'm not resting until he's dead.

"Mmmuugh."

"How about this. Grunt once if you're surrendering."

"Unh." If I was able to speak, that grunt would be the word "die," but it'll have to do.

"Excellent. Load him up. Try not to damage him any more, please."

That fake cordiality always pisses me off. People who do that sort of thing like to pretend they're refined, like violence isn't enjoyable but a necessary evil. They're always the sickest psychos.

My shoulders ache and my legs won't work. It takes three of them to drag me to the SUV and push me inside. Even if I could get signals to my extremities, I wouldn't. Passive aggression is all I can manage, so it's what I'm going to do.

There's not much I can do from the back seat I'm draped over, but I hope Zero is having better luck. Of course she is. How else would she be doing? If anyone went after her, it wasn't more than one, and she can outsmart them. I wouldn't be surprised if she won the fight, but that's not really her style, and I don't wish any more violence in her life.

The rumble of an engine starts.

"You two, go find the girl, see why Emek hasn't gotten her back yet."

She's still free. Emek is a younger vampire, maybe four hundred years old or so. Impatient, brash, and prone to giving up. I couldn't have asked for a better adversary for her. By the time whoever the other two are catch up, she'll be gone.

That leaves Costecu and four others with me. Costecu won't drive. He'd never stoop to something so menial and common, and he's not going to share seats with anyone either, so he'll be in the front passenger seat. Getting past the others to grab and snap his neck has a low probability of working, as tempting as it is. My time would be better spent recovering.

It might've been the longest drive ever or the shortest. Things start to twitch back to life on the way while my brain is occupied with thoughts of what Zero is doing. When she evades the people after her, she's an hour drive from the city. She has no car and enough smarts not to go back to the cabin. She doesn't strike me as the outdoorsy type. It'll probably take her a day or two to get back if she walks. I can hold out for much longer than that.

The dull blobs of the interior of the SUV coalesce into more defined blobs of the floor of the SUV. I'm able to turn my head and peer at the back of the seat in front of me. Three heads rise above it, crammed together in space meant for two. Craning back, the light from the tinted window blinds me, but I blink and blink, not giving up until my eyes focus. The top of the occasional tree blots out the sun.

I'm registering more discrete sounds instead of the background buzz of everything smashed together: the wheels on the pavement, the quiet sounds of some Baroque composer I can't be bothered to know, people shifting in their seats, and my own labored breathing.

I'm pretty sure I've got a punctured lung. That means my ribs are worse than I thought. They'll heal, over time by themselves. Costecu isn't going to do anything to help. If I had to guess, he'll toss me somewhere to rot while my body recovers.

I experiment with wiggling toes. It takes a few false starts, but then they respond. The pain burns, but pain means feeling, and feeling means they're still there. It's a step in the right direction. My next attempt is moving the hand and arm not trapped under my body.

Out the window, trees turn to buildings. We'll be back to base soon. I have no illusions I'll be able to do anything serious by then, but you never know. It can't hurt to be prepared. By the time the buildings turn to warehouses and darkness descends as we drive underground to the base's garage, I'm able to curl my fingers into a loose fist.

The SUV stops, the doors open, and I'm dragged out into the familiar underground space where I spent most of my time when I wasn't out following orders and causing mayhem. The cabin was the only retreat I had. There's no way I can go back. I wouldn't be surprised to find it burned to the ground out of spite.

Giving them no help at all, I go limp and force them to drag me. I don't give Costecu the satisfaction of noticing him when he stands in front of me with his polished black dress shoes.

"Are you capable of speech yet?"

It's a good question, but I'm not giving him the satisfaction of finding out. From here on out, I give nothing.

"I see." The tone in his voice is calm, but the undertone of irritation is unmistakable. He wants to be able to lord his superiority over me proving he won. After a few moments of silence with me keeping my head down and my mouth shut, he lets out a short sigh. "Very well. Put him in the cells."

His shoes disappear and I'm being dragged again. The anger of the people hauling me is clear from the way I'm bumped into walls and slammed through doors.

The environment fostered in a place like this is competitive, as in brutal. Any bit of weakness is beaten out, with strength being the path to the top. Now I'm enemy number one, there's a power vacuum. Everyone's going to want a shot at me to prove I'm not strong and they are.

One of my shoulders is released, a door opens, and they attempt to throw me inside. I may be incapacitated, but it's not easy to throw a seven-foot body anywhere. I let myself tumble to the stone floor. No point in giving them anything. My plan is to stay quiet and don't move until they're gone. If I don't react to anything, they'll get bored and leave like adorable kittens.

I take the first of what I expect will be many beatings. They punch and kick me some more, but the pain doesn't add much to what I'm already feeling. It's like putting more ketchup on fries. At some point it's all ketchup. It's been a while since I had fries or ketchup. Not going to get any of that in here. That'll be the first thing I do when I get out. Well, Zero will be the first thing I'll do, and then fries and ketchup. Maybe a hamburger afterwards. Then Zero again.

They must've stopped at some point during imagining Zero and fries, because things are back to dull pain instead of sharp pain. I listen for a while to learn if they're still in the room, but it doesn't seem like it.

Recovery might take longer than normal. I have to expect getting pummeled is going to be a regular occurrence.

I don't like not being in control, but there's always something you can do to improve your life, no matter what the situation. I can't control people coming in to beat me up yet, but I can control how much it'll hurt.

Bit by bit bodily functions come back online. My arms start to burn, really burn, like they've been set on fire. Dragging myself to a wall and pulling my body up so I'm not flat on the floor, I examine my wounds in the dark of the cell.

Several fingers are broken, toes too no doubt. My left shoulder is dislocated. Something is definitely wrong with my left knee. Dried blood is all over my exposed skin, thick like ketchup—some fries right now would be so good—and I can't tell where the cuts are. There's not going to be any water forthcoming to help me clean or disinfect, never mind quenching my thirst.

All I can do is sit in the dark and wait for my body to rebuild itself. I'll help it along as much as I can. Eat and drink whatever they bring me, if they bring me anything. Rest while I can to conserve energy. I'll get out of here by myself if I can.

I shove down the guilt at asking Zero to rescue me. I shouldn't've put her in that position. I should've ordered her to leave and go somewhere else. In the heat of the moment, I wasn't thinking. To be more accurate, I wasn't thinking with my brain. I want her back, but if I have to stay locked up here the rest of my life it'd be okay knowing she's safe.

Resolve helps dampen the pain as I push upright to standing. The more my blood flows, the faster things will heal. I need to keep moving and get back to fighting shape as quickly as possible to get myself out of here before she does something rash and gets captured.

The thought of her back in these cells makes me sick to my stomach. It'd be all my fault. If she gets hurt in any way, I'll have failed her. I can't live with that.

Little crackles in my toes accompany shooting pain as I start to walk around the room. My knee doesn't want to bend, but I force it with my hands. I've felt my own bones grinding against each other before, and while it's not pleasant, it's not unexpected. It won't stop me from healing and achieving my goals.

After about an hour of me hobbling in a circle in the empty stone cell, things are still painful, but movement is smoother. All my joints are throbbing like the center of the sun, hot and urgent. Good thing I don't care. I can get new joints. I can't get a new Zero.

The door opens, splashing in dim grey light, which does nothing to illuminate the space. Looks like I've got more visitors.

CHAPTER THREE

Aideen

Convinced I've lost whatever pursuer I had, I crawl out from under the leaves, stand, and take stock. I'm in the middle of the woods, thirty plus minutes of running away from the highway, and I have no shoes. Tugging at the collar of Lindberg's dress shirt to cover my shoulder, which keeps peeking out, I'm worried a bear might see me and get the wrong idea. I spin in a slow circle.

Trees on all sides, and it's afternoon-ish. The sun is almost directly overhead, and I have no idea which way is east. Isn't there a saying about moss growing on the north side of trees? I check a few but find no directional consensus from what moss colonies there are.

I guess I'll start walking in as much of the opposite direction of from where I came as possible and try to watch where the sun is going. After five minutes I stop and reevaluate my course of action. The most important thing is to find civilization. If I go back the way I came, they'll be waiting for me. I drove west out of the city to get near Drew's cabin, and then he drove us north, so if I head south, I should hit the main highway at some point. South might be this way.

Provided I don't get a weirdo who thinks these loose clothes are an invitation, I should be able to get a ride back. If he does get ideas, I'll knock him out and steal his car. I'm a veteran car thief. I can't help but laugh to myself before switching to hoping the woman whose car I stole got it back.

A bird titters overhead and a squirrel darts through the undergrowth as I turn to walk in a theoretical southward direction. If my guess at distance is correct, which I doubt since I've never been good at that sort of thing, we drove about thirty miles north, so I have to walk thirty miles south. If I can somehow walk at a steady pace through the woods, it'll take a little less than eight hours to get there. Easy.

By that time, they'll have gotten Drew back to their base and pulled out every single one of his toenails, no doubt. Dwarves don't have the same type of regeneration selkies do. Their blood clots much quicker than normal, and bones can heal within hours, but I'm not sure if toenails would grow back right away. They aren't bone. Would his teeth grow back?

I lean against a tree as a wave of dizziness passes over me. I'm hungry and thirsty, and I can't stand the thought of Drew being tortured. He bought my freedom with his pain. There's no way I'll let him suffer for me. That kind of debt is too much to bear.

The bark is rough against my cheek, the scent of dirt is a subtle undertone to everything, and the sun has moved to my right. I'm headed in the correct direction at least. If he can fight off seven people long enough for me to flee like a coward, I can walk eight hours to get to the highway.

The sun moves down the curve of the sky, the shadows of the trees stretch out and mingle together, and bird chirping blends with cricket noises. My feet, protected only by socks, are in a world of hurt. I don't want to stop and examine how bad the damage is, so I'm left to imagine the blisters and bleeding.

Taking several breaks on the way helps. During one of them I find a sharp rock and cut off the bottom of the slacks to somewhere mid-calf, leaving them a jagged mess along the bottom. Lindberg might get pissed, but I'm tired of tripping over the cuffs every time they unroll.

The next break I find another rock and tear the stitches out of the shoulders of the sleeves, discarding them as well. I bet I look like the world's most fashionable survivalist in a three-hundred-dollar button-up. I can't figure out a way to keep the neck from sliding off one shoulder or the other, which irritates me more than it should. It gives me something to focus my attention on instead of walking.

I can do this. It's only walking. People walked everywhere before cars. Or horses. I'm in shape. Eight hours is nothing.

The constant repetition of cheering myself on is annoying and distracting, getting me where I need to go. There's nothing else to focus on. While untouched woodland has a certain beauty, it's also boring. Trees are trees, leaves are leaves, and I'm sure the same damn bird has been following me the whole time. The occasional patch of thick bushes I have to navigate around, or a sharp rock that assaults my wounded feet, are the only breaks in the monotony.

I pass the time by trying to figure out why I'd been shot at by my colleagues when I'd managed to escape from Costecu the first time. I'd expected relief and questions, but instead I got bullets before I even made it in the front door. Why they'd come at me is a mystery unsolved, and one I'll need to figure out.

Absorbing in such mysteries and the darkening day, I almost walk into the rising hill of gravel in front of me. I stumble to a stop stubbing my toe on a large stone.

"Fuck."

After shaking off the pain, I glance up. A sound caught my attention. A car. The highway must be up the hill. My trek is over. Have I been walking eight hours? Aches in my thighs, and numbness in my calves tell me I have. I look down to make sure my feet are still there.

I scramble up the rockslide to the top, and the sight of the highway sends a flood of relief through me in a way the mere sound did not. The problem is I'm on the north side, and I need to be on the south to head back into the city.

It's early night, dusk turned into twilight, but there are still cars. It's not as empty as when I drove up it at 3 am. I doubt anyone can see me lurking on the side of the blacktop. Until I want attention, it's better that way.

An appropriate size gap in cars shows up without needing to wait much and I hobble across the three lanes and down into the drainage ditch between the north and southbound lanes.

It's wet and muddy, which is helpful because it cools my feet. They've been burning, but I hadn't noticed, during my trek. As the burn drops from off-the-register pain back to more normal on-fire pain, I have to sit for a minute.

I've abused these socks more than they deserve, yet they're still intact. I should get a few pairs when I get back. I wonder if Drew remembers where he got them. He might. Seems to be a pretty fashionable guy.

Biting back a laugh, a small weight lifts off my shoulders. The last thing I should be doing is wondering about his style sense while sitting in a puddle of mud between the lanes of a highway. I'm almost home. It's only the first step, but it's going to be so good to change out of these clothes and back into my own. After I take a bath. Ten or fifteen extra minutes won't change anything. I hope.

Struggling up, my hands sinking into the muck, I climb the shallow bank. I can walk toward home and maybe someone will pick me up, torn clothes, mud, and all.

Cars pass ignoring or not seeing me. This is the second time in less than a week I've tried to hitchhike somewhere in the middle of the night. Last time I was missing a toenail and had no shoes, but my clothes fit. I'm not sure which scenario is worse. Either way my feet lose. At least my toenail grew back in Drew's shower.

This walk has the potential to be much longer. When I escaped Costecu's hideout I had to trek only across the city, but this time it's a sixty-mile hike. Being able to walk on flat ground and not dodge trees, rocks, and squirrels is an improvement, but the distance is not.

I question whether I can walk another ten hours after the eight I just did, all without stopping for more than five minutes or sleeping. My muscles say I can't, so to override them I start singing.

The last time I sang out loud was that karaoke night way back when I was still on the human police force, and my friends had tried to convince me to get a tattoo. I've been too busy to do much of anything since my promotion and recruitment into The Organization. Karaoke was a month before transferring to my current job, and then two more months when I got put in charge of tracking down Costecu and Drew.

The lyrics for "Purple Rain" spring to mind and drop from between my lips slow and hesitating. It's an awkward thing to sing to yourself in the middle of the night on the side of a highway. Soon, all sense of proprietary is gone. There's no better time or place. No one's around, there aren't any phones to take compromising videos, and I can pretend I'm not off-key.

One song leads to the next, which leads to the next. There might be some Backstreet Boys in there, but I refuse to shame myself about it. As I'm belting out the chorus to "Love Shack," a passing car puts on their brakes, accelerates, and then brakes again, pulling over onto the shoulder. I shut my mouth.

Resisting the urge to run up to it, because it might spook whoever's driving, and it might be one of Costecu's people, I slow my pace. Whoever it is waits about a quarter mile down the highway, and so far, no doors have opened. It's possible they're a murderer or rapist hoping to catch me off-guard, but if so, they'll be in for a rude surprise. I might've been walking for over eight hours, but years of being a detective and then an investigator have left me with pretty good instincts. Plus, I've got a strong jaw and a mean right hook.

Halfway there, both the driver and passenger side doors open. My heart stutters, because I'd be outnumbered if it's a murdering couple. I might not have the energy to fight off both of them. I'm being paranoid.

"Hey there, hon, you okay?"

The voice is convivial, female, and motherly. Odds are, not a killer. But I shouldn't let my defenses down yet. There have been middle-aged women who were killers. There's still another person who hasn't shown themselves.

"Yes. I'm okay," I fib. I don't want to end up at a hospital or police station because these people decide what's best for me. Trying to invent a story to explain my situation would be much more difficult to a fellow law-enforcement officer. "Could use a ride, though."

The other figure on the passenger side is a male. Both of them are older. Not many retirement-age murdering married couples in the history of crime. I'm exhausted enough to take my chances.

"How far ya goin'?"

"Into the city. You can drop me anywhere."

I'm only a handful of feet from their back bumper, and I stop. I don't want to frighten off my ride. They should be more afraid of me than the other way around. I must look crazy and homeless. I could be on drugs or a hardened car thief.

The man is eyeing me with caution, but the woman gestures to the door, ignoring his obvious discomfort. "We're goin' there, too. We can take ya, hon. Drop you off at...wherever you want to go?" Her eyebrows raise at the question.

No matter how nice they appear, I'm not giving them my address. I don't want to go back to base yet, because of what happened last time I showed up. Somewhere a few blocks from my condo would be ideal. There are a lot of condos and apartments in the area. They wouldn't know which one is mine. "The corner of

Fifth and Pine would be great. But wherever you want is fine. I don't want to impose."

"Naw, you ain't imposin', dear. Be glad for the company."

The man grumbles at the edge of my hearing but says nothing else.

"Thank you so much," I say, allowing a smidgen of relief to temper my caution. Opening the door to a well-used but cared for sedan, I slip onto the back seat. In the brief light of the overhead lights, before the doors shut and the woman heads back to the highway, I get a glimpse of my appearance.

Muddy, dirty, ragged. Hands scratched and dry. I've left a muddy skid across the upholstery. I tug a stick out of my hair, and, not sure what to do with it, twiddle it between my fingers.

The man stares straight ahead, but the woman glances at me in the rearview mirror. "So whatcha doin' out in the middle of nowhere, lookin' like ya haven't bathed in a week?"

I can't tell her anything near the truth. "You wouldn't believe me."

"We got an hour, hon. Got nothin' else to do."

This is to be the price of my ride, then. I was hoping to maybe nap, but it appears not. I start spinning a tale of a camping trip gone wrong. First I lost my cell phone in a creek, then my friends ran off and left me when a bear showed up in the middle of the night. While I was curled in a fetal position to avoid drawing attention from the bear, it shredded all my clothes when searching through my bag. The only thing left was this shirt and pants from my now very ex-boyfriend. I made sure to sound extra angry at that part.

It's not all that plausible, but if they doubt it, they don't show it. She listens with interest, interjecting with a question every few minutes, and he falls asleep against his window with a snore.

At least manufacturing a story passes the time. Before too long the lights of the city appear and crest the horizon, an orange beacon of civilization. Traffic increases, and then we're flowing along with all the other night-time drivers. It isn't that late, only a little after ten according to the car clock, and Friday as well. It feels good to be surrounded by people who are, odds on, human instead of something supernatural like me.

"Here we are, hon," Darla says. I've learned that Darla and Vernon moved here a year ago to be closer to their grandchildren, and that he hates the cold and she's discovering espresso. "Are you sure we can't take you somewhere else?"

"Nope, this is exactly where I want to be. Thank you for the ride. You'll have a good story to tell your family."

"That we will. Good luck, dear. You give that young man a talking to," she adds, waving her finger as they pull away.

The towers of downtown loom over me, bathed in white and orange light. A two-minute walk and I'll be home. The other people out and about avoid meeting my gaze, and I can't say I blame them.

Each step brings out new pains and sores, but I push them away. There's the main entrance for my building. The familiar color light spilling out onto the sidewalk is a metaphorical bath to my soul. I push open the doors and step inside, scraggly hair, jagged clothes, and all.

"Miss Duffy." the doorman exclaims, face breaking from his normal welcoming smile into a shocked expression. "Are you all right?"

"Hi Salvador. Yes, I'm fine. I had an adventure. Um, I've lost my key, can you let me in?"

"Of course, Miss Duffy. Do you need me to call anyone?"

"No, thank you."

He watches me with concern but says nothing on the ride up the elevator. Down the hall and around the corner is my condo. The key clicks into the lock where it belongs, and then he pulls it out without turning the knob.

"Please, let me know if you need anything, okay?" he asks, radiating concern.

"Thank you, Salvador. I will. I promise."

He turns and walks away, and I wait until the elevator dings before opening my door and stepping inside.

Home. The lights are off, as they should be. Everything is silent. Home, and a bath. All my tension drains away and lays in a puddle on the floor. Dragging myself to my bedroom and the bath I need and want, I flick on the light beside my couch.

"Hello, Aideen."

I stumble, catching myself on the couch. "Jackson? What are you doing here?"

"I'm doing what's needed." He stands up from the chair.

The cold flash of metal on the barrel of the gun wakes me up faster than any bath ever could.

CHAPTER FOUR

Druain

I fend off the attack without too much trouble. Clearly, they thought they were going to do more damage. I want to beat the shit out of them, but later, when I can breathe without pain.

After my attackers leave, I take stock again. I have a couple more broken ribs. I wouldn't be surprised to learn they wore steel-toed shoes on purpose. Pushing back to my feet and leaning against the wall for support, I start my uneven circle around the room once more.

Some people might distract themselves by talking out loud, but being a double agent for a long time has made me cautious. If I have to be careful not to say anything out of character, I have to be extra careful with what I keep to myself. Thoughts shape actions.

I guess it doesn't matter anymore. I'm not sure if Costecu believes I've been working with the opposition, but attempting to run away with a member of the opposition, thereby depriving him of a toy and making him look foolish, is bad enough. He's not going to let me live no matter what he believes.

Which is fine. He can plan anything he wants, because I'm getting out of here and killing him on the way. If I don't escape, if I can take him out, it'll make a world of difference. Zero will be safe, for one thing. I guess a lot of other people would be too. But it's not so much about them anymore.

Guilt about who it used to be about bobs to the surface. I clench my jaw and push it away. While there was good reason to take this assignment, it's not a healthy reason. Not if I want to stay alive and see Zero again. Going in, I hadn't planned to come back out, but I'd kind of like to. I'd say it's fifty-fifty.

There are definite perks to Zero. The poking, the teasing, the indignant growls. The tits, those legs: I bet she's a biter. The way she gnawed on Gil's neck when trying to distract him. Right through the scales. Actually, that makes me a bit nervous. I swallow and adjust my pants.

However, if an opportunity presents itself to kill Costecu, even if it means I take myself out in the process, I have to do it. There have been chances before, but I wanted to make sure we got everyone in this cell. By this point, I'm more interested in pure revenge. He hurt Zero. He wants to keep hurting her, and I won't let anyone else get killed because I waffled. The anger helps me keep moving while my bones and organs work at stitching themselves back together.

The sounds of the other prisoners have always been background noise, and I notice them now because they've gone quiet. No one is moaning or groaning or crying. Something's up. Maybe they want to know what'll happen to me next.

As if on cue, footsteps ring out across the stone. More visitors. I'm not ready, but when will I ever be? Not any time soon at this rate. There's never going to be a perfect moment, because Costecu won't give me the time to heal.

I stand on the far side of the cell, opposite the doorway, and wait. Hiding off to the side would make them suspicious, and it wouldn't give me momentum I need. When they open the door and see me, for that split second they'll relax, because I'm where I should be.

The door opens inward, a sliver of light growing like the crack of dawn, my opening to danger. Because I'm going right for Costecu. Broken bones or not, I have to try.

I start running, driving my legs forward before the door opens all the way or I can tell who's on the other side. Clipping my shoulder on the still opening door, I use the momentum to twist and slam into the people on the other side, knocking them down like pins in a bowling alley.

The satisfying meaty thunk of bodies hitting the wall is food to my aching muscles and cramping joints. A blow hits me in the back of the head. I've got nothing but my instincts and reactions, dulled as they are, but I make it work.

Fights don't typically last long, even though when I'm in them it feels like forever. Not more than thirty seconds later my erstwhile assailants are in a pile on the floor. My ears are ringing from the punch in the head, but that's a minor issue, far down the list of concerns.

As I'm catching my breath, I'm struck with an idea. All these prisoners might be helpful. I imagine most are angrier at Costecu than I am. Several are plain crazy, and one or two would rather attack me than attempt freedom.

I start breaking off door handles. It's not as easy the time I did it for Zero so she could escape. That was an open and unlocked door, and I was as close to full strength as I've been in a while. Some of these have been closed for a while, with only the little slots for food trays getting any use. Hinges might be frozen, but I'll do what I can.

The ring of metal on stone as old-fashioned handle after handle hit the floor is a clear alarm for anyone who's listening, but I can't be bothered to care too much. I'm not being cautious at all, but my body is teetering on the edge of shutting down. If I stop, everything is going to seize up. I don't bother opening the doors. Anyone too far out of touch to understand what's going on won't be much help.

Down the line I go. They had me at the furthest cell, where the passageway stopped. The cell where the back wall was wet from natural stone and no bed survived long because of mold and mildew. As I go, creaks and footsteps echo around the small spaces, letting me know people are rousting themselves.

"Here's the deal," I shout, not worried about caution anymore. I'm too tired, fed up, and pissed off. "Do whatever you want, as long as it's not trying to take me out. Go free, stay here and kill everyone, I don't care. This is the only chance you'll get, and if you get caught, they'll probably kill you, so...good luck."

I stop at the last one and grab the handle, leaning against the wall to catch my breath. I haven't been able to snap the last few off, as my reserves falter, caught between self-healing and exertion. All I've got to do is get to Costecu. Shuffling tells me ex-prisoners are approaching, waiting, assessing. I spin and glare at the motley lineup of psychos, innocents, and tortured creatures.

"Go on. I'm not fucking leading you or anything. Get out of here," I say, flinging my hand toward the only exit. There are already reinforcements coming. All the sound has not escaped notice.

One of them steps forward, a young werewolf. I remember capturing him. He eyes me, the decision of what to do warring plainly on his face. After another moment he growls, and then springs forward, past me and toward the approaching people here to put everyone back.

I don't let out the breath I had been holding because my lungs wouldn't be happy with the rapid exhalation. The rest of them start to tumble forward, a rockslide building up steam. There're not many, maybe twenty or so, but it should be enough for my purpose.

I let them crash ahead and tangle with the outnumbered guards. Shouts ring out, bones break, flesh tears. Someone hits the alarm, and the lights start to flash red. The siren sounds in the distance, hollow and loud, bouncing off each rock surface of Costecu's underground lair.

I've got to get past them and out to the throne room where Costecu is no doubt holed up, or about to be. He'll crouch down in his private room off of it, waiting for his peons to clean up whatever mess is going on. Putting down prison breaks isn't the job of someone as "cultured" as he is. Let the commoners fight among themselves. An ingrained attitude from the century in which he was born.

Without his involvement, my mini rebellion will survive longer than if he did the proactive thing and led the counter attack. He might not be able to shut it down by himself, but he's fast, strong, and can create a lot of damage. If I'd been serious about my job, I would've tried to train the passiveness out of him.

Shoving past fighting bodies, throwing an elbow or knee where applicable, I drag myself past the melee. The prisoners will win this battle, but there're enough people in the garrison to grind down the uprising. The smart ones will do what I'm doing and try to push past the fighting to get to the one way out of here. The elevator that goes up to the surface.

I'm betting on it being guarded, which will take some people away from being near Costecu.

Free of the largest part of the fighting, which is spilling out to along the corridors, I jog and limp my way to the main room off of which Costecu's audience chamber, throne room, however he wants to style it, is located.

Before I can get there a group of people rush at me.

"The prisoners have escaped, go get them," I shout, gesturing back behind me and rushing forward like I'm going somewhere important. Maybe not everyone knows I'm supposed to be a prisoner.

I have no such luck. The leading person grabs at me. "Hey. You're the traitor."

I start swinging. There are six of them, and the hallway isn't narrow enough for me to take only one at a time. In five seconds, I'm surrounded, with nowhere to go, and the only way out is if I can put them all on the floor. I succeed at getting one down, knocking his head against the wall by pushing back against him, but then hands grab at me.

As I'm grappling with an antagonist in front of me, fearing this is the end of my plans, the weight of the person hanging off my back is torn away with a scream and ripping flesh. The one I'm fighting is momentarily distracted, opening up the opportunity for me to slug him in the throat. Much softer than hitting someone in all the hard bones of their face, and a lot more effective.

There's chaos around me. Shouts, grunts, more noises of people hitting and being hit. I'm jostled forward, pushed to the side, swept over by a handful of the prisoners I'd let out, led by that young werewolf. He gives me a look somewhere between *thanks* and *get out of my way* as his posse crashes past.

Taking a second to catch my breath, I follow. They'll be a useful distraction, whether they succeed or not. Subtlety is out of the question at this point, so I might as well let them charge ahead and distract everyone, allowing me to sneak my way along in their wake.

They make good time, although they meet increasing resistance along the way. I hang back and watch from the shadows. If I can avoid fighting, that'll only help. Costecu isn't going to be a pushover, and those dull aches in my bones aren't getting any better.

One or two prisoners fall along the way, either knocked out or dead. For the most part, they come out better than most of the guards they meet. The motivators of freedom and revenge are stronger than the motivation of fighting because someone's paying you. There's going to be a fair number of opposing forces who won't show up at all, tucking themselves away into a dark corner. It's not too surprising we make it to the main hall without meeting massive resistance.

There is resistance in the mail hall, and they have weapons. I'm glad for my escorts as they go charging in without a care, allowing me to peel off and sneak to the other side of the wide hall. Shadows and chaos help me stay undetected as I slink the length of the room. Clashing combatants sounds from behind me as I step up to the large doors behind which are Costecu and his medieval office.

They may be locked, they may be guarded, but I can't be hanging around trying to decide what to do. I've got to catch him by as much surprise as possible if I'm going to have any hope of saving Zero, and of escape. I rear back to attempt to smash the door in, then pause. I'd like to spare my shoulder additional pain if possible, so I reach for the knob and turn it. The door opens.

I slam it open the rest of the way, and I'm rewarded by a satisfying meaty thunk and groan as whoever was behind it is flattened against the wall. Striding in, surveying the area, there's no sign of Costecu. His chair is empty, his bookshelves are unattended, his writing desk has the lamp turned off. He must be in his private chambers.

Five quick steps and I'm at the door to it, hand on the ornate handle, and pushing it open.

"Mr. Lindberg," Costecu says, smiling at me from his Victorian wingback. His fingers are steepled.

I charge.

The chair splinters under my weight as I come crashing down on it, but he's no longer in it.

"Must we resort to violence?" he asks from my left, as if there's ever been any other answer to problems.

I leap up and charge at him again, but once more he's out of the way with a speed I can't track. I get a cuff upside my head, like you'd give to a puppy who keeps trying to bite your ankles. It's sends me smashing into the corner post of his bed.

"I won't ask again," he intones.

At this point it doesn't matter. I'd thought and hoped I could pull it off. End this whole horrible corruption. A rotten tooth with Costecu at the core, a tumor in my soul. The recent dream of cutting out the blight before it could infect Zero is turning into a nightmare.

I've lost. I know it, he knows it, and it doesn't make a bit of difference what I do.

Things aren't going to go my way in the near future. I'll be around long enough to have a distant future, too, but it's not going to be a happy one. I lurch around and make another run at him.

Zero would be disappointed if I gave up without giving it my all, no matter how futile.

This time he doesn't need to use his speed to get out of the way. He grabs my wrist in an iron-like hold and pivots, swinging me around him, a star crashing into a black hole. I hit the floor face-first, and then he's on top of me, twisting my arm hard against my back.

He can't weigh more than a hundred-fifty pounds, but I might as well be buried under solid rock. I couldn't get up even if I was in the best of shape. As it is, I'm bruised, bloody, and all the broken bones I'd been ignoring ignite in pain.

"It didn't have to be this way," he whispers in my ear, like the world's worst lover.

"It was always going to be this way," I growl back.

Colors explode in my vision, growing to dark spots as unconsciousness hits me with all the speed of death.

CHAPTER FIVE

Aideen

"What's going on, Jackson?" I raise my hands, a natural defensive posture when faced with a gun. His hand is steady, his stare burrowing into me.

"Sorry, chief. You're a mess that needs cleaning up."

His hand isn't shaking, but he's not shooting yet. I don't have a ton of experience with having a gun pulled on me, but it's happened, and I do know a lot about people and how they act. I didn't get to be a detective for the police, and then head my own supernatural task force, because of my looks.

"What do you mean?" I keep my voice steady, switching over into calm interrogation mode. The longer I can keep him talking, the better chance I have and the more I'll know. While he's deciding on an answer, I'll be thinking of a way out.

"You don't need to know."

"Is someone paying you?" Lifting a foot, I slide it over a few inches. The couch is between us, but maybe I can slip over so it's not. Then I might have a chance to dodge, or duck, or get at him in one way or another. It's not a great plan, but it's all I have.

"No. Well, yes," he rolls his free hand in a "that's not the point" gesture. "It's about more than money."

I'm inching to my right, one slow step after another. One thing I won't have to worry about is the socks sliding out from under me on the hardwood floor. They're so scuffed and dirty I could get traction on glass. There's almost no bottom left to them. Jackson's eyes flick down when he notices what's going on. "You want to shoot me because of an ideal?" I ask, attempting a moment of distraction.

"I want to be free. Stop moving." The last sentence is punctuated by a wiggle from the barrel of the gun.

Jackson has been a soldier for almost all of his life. He joined the army at eighteen, then the police force, moved to SWAT, and we recruited him to lead our teams. There's not much I can do he hasn't seen before. If I can upset him, maybe I can throw him off-balance enough to try something, but as tired and aching as my muscles are, it's not good odds for me either way.

The only thing I can do is roll the dice.

"I've been walking for eight hours, Jackson. Eight hours through a forest. That was after running for thirty minutes with Costecu's goons behind me. I'm tired. If you don't let me sit down I might fall over." I stop moving while talking, but when I finish, I raise my eyebrows a touch and start to shift over to the right again.

His face hardens as he scans the mess I am. Tattered and dirty clothing that isn't mine. Dirty, sweaty, I must smell terrible. I lift a foot to show him I'm not wearing any shoes. "These socks used to be white." Any concession I can get is the start of more concessions. Standard technique, and I'm sure he's aware of it, but it's standard for a reason.

After a moment, he backs into the hallway where the rest of my condo is, keeping well out of reach, but also in a good sight line, and nods. "Fine. Sit. Don't try anything else."

I creep around the couch, watching in case he tries anything. As if I could stop him. The light I turned on throws a white pool on the carpet and a smaller one onto the ceiling. As I pass by it blanks out my night vision, leaving spots behind so I can't see Jackson's face. I don't want to sit down, it was only an excuse, but I have no choice. I ease onto the cushions, a little put off that the throw pillows aren't straight.

He lets me sit. If he wanted to shoot me, he would have already, so something is holding him back. My vision clears and I can see him again. Standing stock straight, the gun still pointed at me, not leaning against the wall at his back. Despite appearing to be in control of the situation, he's not relaxing like an amateur would.

"Free from what?" I ask.

He snorts, as if the answer is obvious. "Please. Like you don't feel the same way."

"I don't know what you're talking about." I suspect I do, but it would solidify what fears I have to get him to say it out loud. It's not a good idea to assume things, no matter how obvious they are.

"Everything. Hiding. Not being who I am. The jokes."

"Jokes? What jokes?" I rest my hands on my knees.

He grumbles a little, like he doesn't want to talk about this. "Like the short jokes, for example. You know how much that adds up over the years? I'm five foot five. It's not like I'm a midget or anything."

I doubt the jokes are the main reason, but maybe they're the straw that broke his back. I can't see him doing this because someone called him short. I adopt a casual tone, another attempt to lower the tension in the room. "I get that. I'm almost six feet. I've been that way since I was twelve. I towered over all the girls at school. It's part of life."

"That's not...you act like that's all it is. It's not." He takes a step as if to start pacing, but then corrects himself and stills. "Every day, all I see are humans and what they do to each other. They're all so dumb. Killing, lying...ruining everything."

This is starting to sound familiar. Propaganda disseminated by Costecu and his ilk. Point out all the flaws humans have, and then show how he's so much better. "You can solve that by killing me?" I make sure not to mask my incredulity.

It's a provocation, for sure, but I don't have many levers to push in this situation. I've got to use what I can. If there's the smallest percentage I can piss him off enough to lower his guard, I have to try.

"Don't try to bait me," he replies, switching the gun to the other hand. "It's not about you. I mean, it is right now because you're helping them, and you know where...well. You know stuff."

"I know a lot of stuff," I agree. "But so do a lot of other people. Are you going to kill them too?"

He scoffs. "Once I'm done with you and Lindberg disappears, it'll be easy to paint you as a traitor or a double agent or something. Anything you've learned since he grabbed you isn't leaving this room."

The brief flash of anger I'd been stoking in him snuffs out. He's in control of his emotions. I need to find another tactic. Going back in the conversation to try to piss him off again is a clear sign I'm up to something. He'll stop talking, and then I'm done for. "How long have you been working for Costecu?" Might as well ask the obvious question and get it out of the way.

He chuckles a little. "Do you think I'm a supervillain or something? I'll reveal everything, keep talking, so you can get a chance to escape? Not happening. None of your business." He moves the gun back to his right hand, no doubt in preparation of pulling the trigger.

Being flexible in conversations is one reason I'm good at my job. Conversations are like fights: you have to take what your opponent says and adjust your tactics. "So why haven't you shot me yet?" Changing gears again, I'm hoping if I can get him to think about taking the shot and actually killing me, he'll change his mind. It's a slim hope, but if he won't let me draw him into anger, there're not a lot of other options open to me.

If he were a human, I might be able to jump up and take him on. They're a little slower, a little less decisive. I decide to try it anyway during his answer, but in that split second he must see something in my eyes or the way I move.

He backs up a step, down the hallway, further out of my reach. "Don't even think about it. You're not that dumb. Or fast enough." His eyes go out of focus for a second, as if he's remembering something. Then a slow half-grin creeps over his face. He flicks the tip of his gun up a couple of times, beckoning me.

"What?"

"Get up."

"Why?" I ask but stand up anyway. No use in pissing him off if he's too far away for me to do anything about it.

"Let's go find your thing. Maybe you can be useful and I don't have to kill you. Even though you've been a pain in our asses, and wrong about everything imaginable, I didn't really want to shoot you. I'm not a violent person."

The relief at learning he might not kill me is crushed by the first part of his statement.

Everyone knows the myth around selkies. Seals who turn into women when they shed their seal skin. If you can get your hands on that skin, you can compel her to do your bidding, because she wants her skin back to return to the sea. No real selkie has had to keep a skin for generations, but we all still have some sort of talisman.

When wearing it, we gain more seal-like attributes, and the passive ones we do have, like healing in water and a strong jaw for biting, are enhanced. If it's ever destroyed...well, it would be like losing your soul. I'd have no connection to my past or my community, and that subtle connection to the ocean we all feel would be severed. I've known a poor creature it happened to, and they became a shadow of themself, fading into darkness. One day they simply never got out of bed.

Some keep theirs locked away in bank vaults or hidden in the middle of nowhere. I couldn't bear to be that far from it, and so while I never wear it in public, I keep it in my condo. It feels good to slip it on occasionally, sink into a full tub, and get lost in ancestral memories.

The thought of Jackson, or anyone, getting their hands on my talisman is terrifying. While they wouldn't have actual mind control over me, I'd do almost anything to keep it safe.

"Where's it at?" he asks, wiggling the gun again, as if I need a reminder.

It's in a plain mahogany chest with a simple lock. The talisman is no bigger than a couple of my fingers. I've strung it onto a silver chain so I can wear it as a necklace if need be. The chest has a lock, more for peace of mind than any real security, and I keep the whole thing in my closet, on the bottom shelf, in a cloth basket, underneath old jeans.

The top shelf is too obvious, and people always search women's underwear drawers when they break in. I suspect it's so they can paw at strange panties.

I'm not going to tell Jackson any of this.

"Come on," he growls, setting his jaw in determination. "Tell me where it is."

Gnomes are stubborn, but not as stubborn as dwarves. Once they get a hold of an idea, they don't let go. If they believe you know or have something they want, they're harder to get rid of than oysters off a rock.

"Where what is?" It's a ridiculous question to ask, but I've got to buy any bit of time I can. I start to take slow steps toward him.

He keeps backing down the hallway to my room, keeping the distance between us the same. "Don't be stupid. You know exactly what I mean."

"So then you know I'm not going to tell you."

"Don't be like this. You'd rather me kill you than give it up? Hey, maybe it wouldn't be a great life, but you'd be alive."

Our slow dance continues, me stepping forward and him back, down the length of the hallway. Soon he'll hit the end of the hall. I'm sure he knows that. He's probably scoped out my condo already. He won't let me get any closer.

"I'd rather be dead."

"Tell me where it is." He stops right in front of the wall, keeps a steady look at me, and taps my bedroom door open with his foot. The door swings like silk and he turns sideways to start backing into the room. "Last chance."

"No." I should have waited a few more seconds to get the timing right, but my nerves have been jangling for the last thirty seconds from anticipation of what I'm about to do. I've said no, twice, so he'll either have to keep pushing, or give up. If he keeps pushing, then he starts to lose control since he's asking for something we both know I won't give. If he gives up, that means he has to shoot me, which is something he's doesn't really want to do.

The gun is pointed at me across his body, the first error he's made. Before he can realize the mistake, I leap forward, triggered by the advantage I've been waiting for. That fraction of a second is the best I'm ever going to get. There's no time to pause and calculate how poor my odds are even with this slight edge.

A roar and a flash blind my eyes and deafen ears. My left shoulder explodes in pain, shoved backward by the force ripping through it, but it also spins my right side closer. I grab where I remember the gun being while toppling forward. My hand latches onto something burning hot, hard, and cylindrical.

Shoving the barrel down as hard as I can, ignoring the palm of my hand starting to blister, I half-jump and half-fall against Jackson. I'm taller by six inches, but he's stocky. I use what leverage I can to shove him back, and the gun goes off two more times, roaring into the floor. My hand jerks each time with the recoil, and more waves of hot blast into my palm before it starts to go numb.

We tumble to the floor. Trying to remember anything about the close-quarter combat training I'm mandated to attend once a year, I jab my knees up, trying to find the magical spot. My left arm is burning and tingling, responding half a second slower than it should as I try to grab at his face.

The gun goes off again. My skin is so hot it could be fused to the barrel. I'm shouting in pain, he's shouting in anger, and there's no way I'm going to win this fight if it lasts any longer.

The taste of iron hits my tongue as I bite the side of his neck, instinct finding something to do. He's screaming, and shock washes over me like ice water as I clamp down harder. Twisting, tearing, and chewing, doing my best vampire impression, all focus narrows to my teeth and jaw. Nothing else matters, because everything hinges on this moment.

If I could yell in triumph I would, as with a final twist and gnaw I shred a chunk of skin and blood out of his neck. Another scream and I open my eyes at the same time as I spit out the fleshy, warm hunk of meat.

"You bitch," he slurs, hand flying up to cover the mouth-sized hole in his neck, gun forgotten on the floor as we topple backward, smacking into the frame of my bed. "You bitch."

Thick red blood thumps from between his fingers, spraying the floor and my bed as his head slumps. I have no idea what to say, and I can't tear my stare away as life slips from his body and pools into my carpet.

"That's going to be a huge pain to clean up," I mutter, stifling a frantic laugh. It's easier to contemplate a tiny, mundane detail than all the other more immediate issues. Such as where I killed someone in my apartment, and then there'll be other people coming for me, and how dangerous the whole situation is.

His final gasp of anger and disbelief rings in my ears. His eyes go wide, but then still. His arms slump to the floor and he cants over, smearing more blood across my white duvet. The red doesn't stop flowing.

Dazed, I rock back onto my heels, then stand, reaching out a hand to steady myself against the wall. Pain screams down from my shoulder as I lift it, but for some reason I'm able to ignore it. Adrenaline, probably. My thoughts are hazy, swirling around like noodles in a boiling pot.

I get myself into the bathroom. I need to wash my hands. They're bloody, and I don't want to get an infection. I turn on both taps all the way. My left hand is undamaged, but my right is blackened and blistered in a neat line across the palm. The water stings and burns. I watch as blood sluices away, then black, dead skin, old dirt from under my nails, everything together forming a whirlpool of injured selkie particles.

After about five minutes or so there's nothing left but fresh pink skin where my palm used to be burned. It itches, like it always does.

"You need to take a bath," I say to my reflection. A huge red bloom of my own blood has ruined Lindberg's shirt where I was shot. Somehow that's worse than the bullet hole, or the sleeves I tore off back in the woods.

"Take a bath."

Everything else can wait.

CHAPTER SIX

Druain

I wake up restrained to a chair by thick leather straps across wrists and ankles. It's not the worst way I've ever woken up. That would've been the time I found myself without any shoes, socks, or a shirt at the top of a mountain staring down a cougar. That hadn't ended well. I stopped drinking rum after that.

Still, this isn't pleasant. The leather is too tight, cutting into my circulation, and already my hands are numb. There's almost no light, except for the sick yellow glow from a bare bulb opposite me in the rock wall. As soon as I glance at it, it flicks to full brightness as if sensing my glare, blinding me before I can close my eyes.

I don't need any sight to know there's someone in here with me. Their acrid scent, dry as a frozen mountaintop, is all too familiar. It's Costecu, but I wouldn't've expected anyone else. In fact, I would've been insulted if he'd left this to a lackey.

"How's the breakout going?" I ask to the cool air, attempting to rock the chair, to find if there's any wiggle there. It doesn't budge. Someone must have fixed it.

I didn't expect an answer, and I'm not disappointed when I don't get one. He'll wait for a while, observe and watch, and see if I'll show any signs of weakness. The thing is, I've watched him do all of this. I know every detail of his interrogation technique. I figure he might try something different, but he's too ingrained in his habits. I can use that to my advantage.

Cracking my eyes open a little, letting them adjust to the glare of the bulb, I try to figure out if anything has changed from the last time I was here. Rock walls, a table out of reach with instruments arrayed along it, and a barred window for viewing. All the same as when I had Zero in here. Being in the opposite position hasn't changed anything.

I try a side-to-side movement. Maybe there's some play there. If I can get any little bit of looseness at all, I can exploit it until it becomes a real weakness. Unfortunately, everything is rock solid.

Costecu isn't in my eyesight anywhere, so he must be behind me. He can stay there for all I care. It's not like I'm doing anything unexpected by trying to get out. He knows I would make the attempt, which is no doubt why they've gotten serious about fixing this damn chair to the floor. A quick peek reveals the legs have been sunk into the floor and buried in concrete. When did they find time to do that?

I'm working at trying to free my left wrist, while wiggling my fingers to keep that numb coldness away, when he speaks. "Would you like to keep trying your futile attempts to escape, or would you like to talk?"

His tone is mild, calm, and as dry as his scent and skin. This time it's my turn not to answer, keeping my focus on my task. If I tax my imagination, I can pretend it's giving a millimeter. A whole lot more millimeters and I can pull my wrist out. The burning in my hands is turning to real numbness instead of the fake numbness my brain conjures to tell me something is wrong.

I don't look up as his shadow moves around my left side until he's right in front of me.

"Give me a few more hours to get this hand out and I'll be ready to go," I quip.

He doesn't chuckle, which is good. It means he's super pissed. Emotions are not a good thing for an interrogator to be wrestling with.

His hand shoots out, grabbing the leather binding my wrist and squeezing. I feel some bones shift and crunch a little, but nothing too serious. My jaw clenches, but it's an instinctual reaction, not a real worry about pain.

Then he's undoing the strap. Before I have the opportunity to do something with my freed hand, he's got in his grip again, holding it straight out in front of me. I give a tug, because I have to try, but it's like trying to pull my arm out from granite.

Then the blood rushes back into it. It's the opposite of a great feeling. Burning, ice, buzzing, all the bad things that occur when recovering from having the feeling squeezed out of your extremities.

I grind my teeth so I don't make any noise. That would give him a win.

He slaps the back of my hand, if the word "slap" can be used to describe how hard he hits me. The buzzing turns into a swarm of hornets, burrowing into me with their icy stingers and lava venom. It's shockingly intense. I wouldn't call it pain, not like a red-hot poker in your eye pain, but it's so uncomfortable it makes me wish I didn't have a hand anymore, if only to escape it. It's as if my blood wants to flee my hand, squishing out of every pore.

"Ah, fuck," escapes my mouth, and if I could punch myself, I would.

This is an odd beginning to a torture session, but I can't deny it's an interesting way to start. No physical marks, and it's uncomfortable enough I wouldn't want it to happen again. Do it to the right person a few times, and they'd be in an unstable state.

He slaps my wrist back down onto the chair, sending another jolt of swarming buzzes up to my elbow, and straps it back down. "Hey now, be gentle," I admonish, pushing past the outburst, trying to take the ammunition away from it.

"Why did you do this?" he asks. There's no preamble, another mistake. He's letting me take control.

"I thought you might appreciate it if I delivered myself directly to you, all nice and strapped in and ready to go." I'm not sure if he understands the joke, but it doesn't matter. My tone of voice will tell him how serious I'm not taking this.

"You know how I work," he replies, turning around to walk to the table with the instruments. "I'm sure you don't need to guess what's going to happen if you don't comply."

I do. That makes it easier, in fact. I have no fear of the unknown to worry about, only the certain knowledge of the future. There's going to be a lot of pain, but I've dealt with pain before. I'm not sure if I have an unbroken bone left in my body, but thanks to my dwarf genetics, my bones are pretty solid.

"Tell me what you want, and I'll get right on it," I snap out with a sharp smile. "I'm your dedicated servant. Oh, but you'll have to let me out here first."

He makes a noise between a bat sighing and a lion growling as he picks up a short and thin needle or pin. "So you insist on being insolent."

"If I knew what that fancy word meant, I'd be able to answer." My poking is blatant and transparent, but with the mood he's in, it might work anyway.

He turns around again, gaze fixed on my left hand, and with an easy movement takes my finger and slides the needle under my fingernail. Because my hand is almost back to numb, I don't feel much at first, which gives me a precious few seconds to grab all my reactions and shove them back down. Then the hot bloom, slick and sharp, starts to grow.

It balloons up into a serious problem when he loosens the strap, and feeling and blood rush back into my hand, only to rebound off of the sickening pain rising up from my finger. I've already given him a reaction, so I might as well not worry about it anymore. It'll help spike my adrenaline and take the edge off, too.

"Motherfuck," I bellow. "Whoa, that seriously hurts. We ought to do this to the next prisoner. I bet they'll talk right away." My right hand has been numb this whole time, but muscle memory causes it to clench in sympathetic pain.

Costecu goes back for another needle. He picks it up and comes back without saying anything. His face is as impassive as a marble statue in a museum. The second needle slides in and once again the sick pain roils around my fingertip before coursing up my arm.

"Fuck. All right, all right. I buried the money in my backyard and then poured a concrete porch over it. You could've just asked. Geez." My voice remains steady and uncracked.

To an outsider Costecu would appear to be unaffected by my snark, but I can see the marble façade cracking. An eyebrow moving a millimeter down, a lip parted a fraction of an inch in a snarl. The way he walks back to the bench again, restrained, as if holding himself together. He always wants to pretend he's refined and polite, the model of a gentleman, but underneath he's simply a power-hungry thug who likes to hurt people.

The only way I'm getting out of this is by being dead, or by slipping these bonds. If I can't get any bit of wiggle or jiggle or slip in the leather or the chair, then I'd prefer not to linger here for days and weeks while he pokes and slices at me. That would get boring real fast.

Another needle, another slick jolt of magma pooling in my hand. The buzzing cold from being numb has faded, leaving me to only deal with the sharp needles. Needles aren't too bad.

"Three down, seventeen to go?" I ask. Have to include toes.

"This attitude will get you nowhere." He picks up a ball peen hammer.

"I think it's the chair that's keeping me from going anywhere. How about you let me up?" Blood is pooling under the nails and starting to run down my fingertips.

He still hasn't asked a real question, although I'm not sure what he would learn that he doesn't already know. This is more of a revenge torture session instead of an actual interrogation. It's not going to get better hinging on what I say, unless better means getting knocked out or killed.

The hammer comes down on my index finger like a lightning bolt shattering a tree. I'd managed to keep my pain inside before. I won't be able to anymore. The blunt force of the round hammer combined with the sharp needle still embedded in my skin sets off a whole batch of fireworks in my hand.

My shout trails off into laughter, because there's nothing else I could do. "This is some effective stuff. You're a real professional."

He continues on to smash the next two fingers, then goes back to hit them all a few more times until they're a twisted and bloody mess. It's a relief, because the pain goes from sharp spikes to a dull throbbing. He went too far, ruining them past the point where pain can keep a good foothold. They still hurt, but they're destroyed fingers, not fingers impaled on spikes.

"Hey, so, is this going to take much longer? I'm getting a little hungry. Kind of like to get a bite to eat." Despite my cavalier attitude, the sweat that's formed on my forehead and neck is a reminder this isn't fun.

I spare a moment of thought for Zero. I'm not sure how long I was out, but something tells me it was at least half a day. She should be home. If she does the smart thing, the thing I want her to do, she'll be getting herself right. There's a significant part of me that hopes she leaves and goes somewhere away from all of this fighting and violence to live out her life happily ever after.

Knowing her as much as I do from the few short but intense days we've been together, I doubt she could do that and be happy. With

Costecu still roaming around, she'd never be able to rest. I'd like to think she'd come for me, but even *my* ego isn't that huge.

Costecu is in here, attempting to destroy me, which means he's not out hunting her. I'm buying her time to get everything together and bring him down. Since she's been here, the location isn't secret anymore, and there's nothing from stopping her and all the rest of them from ending this. Costecu is either stupid or arrogant if he believes he can stay and everything will be okay. Does he plan to fight entire specialized strike teams all by himself?

In the end, it doesn't matter. I need to keep him distracted for as long as possible and keep Zero safe. That clicks a switch in my head. I no longer want it to be over. Every second I'm alive, she's alive.

"Let me say, I'm real proud of you," I say, although my tongue feels a bit out of sorts.

Costecu returns to his table, back to me, putting down the hammer and fiddling with his toys. "Whatever do you mean?"

"It's inspiring how you've joined the modern times in terms of interrogation. No more pears, racks, wooden horses, none of that. You've advanced with the times to all those shiny instruments you have there. Much more civilized." My mouth is dry from the adrenaline and lack of hydration. Even though it's only some fingers, non-essential things to start to cut back. It might be fingers now, but who knows what's next.

My answer is apparent when he picks up a heavier hammer. His mouth is drawn into a tight line.

"Aw, c'mon, my hand started feeling better." All the unconscious bodily functions I can't control go into overdrive. My heart races, my palms go sweaty, and my body temperature rises. I know I'll be okay in the long run, but that never makes the short run easier.

He swings the large hammer with ease, bringing it down on top of my knee. The crack is audible under my shout of rage and pain.

"Don't think you broke it," I pant. "Try again, use some muscle thi—"

He smacks my knee again, and this time it does shatter. The splinters of bone spread out from the impact point, knocking all the wind out of my lungs. Not going to be walking on that for a few days. Good thing I'm sitting down.

"It doesn't have to be this way," he says, stepping back one pace and observing.

"Agreed," I growl. "You could let me up and we could deal with this like men."

He laughs his low and breathy chuckle. "Need I remind you that you already tried to attack me and failed miserably?"

"I meant go to a bar and talk it out over some beer. Find some middle ground. Share our feeli—"

He smashes my other knee with the hammer, twice in quick succession, shattering it as well. The lightning supernova that explodes from the point of impact jolts my brain and keeps me awake. Having a high tolerance for pain is helpful when I'm in a brawl, but when I can't do anything about my situation, it's kind of inconvenient. It would speed things along if I could get myself to pass out, but that's not going to happen.

"Gonna need a wheelchair if you wanna get those drinks," I force out of my tight throat.

"You always were such a joker," he says, stepping back for another tool. It's his style. He likes to do lots of things, mix it up, keep it fresh, so I'm not surprised when he picks up the torch. Stabbing, smashing, breaking, now burning.

"Hey, be careful you don't burn my hair, okay? I pay a lot for my haircut."

With a click and woosh the flame leaps out of the nozzle. He spins the adjustment knob with deliberate care, until the flame is thin and blue. It'll have a more concentrated heat, and also do more damage than a wider flame.

Interrogations are a tricky art. Cause too much pain and you're liable to lose the subject. Not enough, and they'll shrug off the questioning. It's obvious he doesn't care about pushing me past the point where I can't answer, so maximum pain is the entire goal.

"Don't worry. I won't hurt your handsome face. I don't want your trollop unable to recognize you when I'm done."

The way he uses the word trollop to refer to Zero makes my blood boil more than all the torture in the world. I wrench and strain at my restraints, uncaring if it's going to show him how much that comment gets to me. He doesn't fail to notice.

"Perhaps she's more than a dalliance?" he asks, one eyebrow arching. "Interesting. I thought perhaps your uncouth coupling was only a product of the stress you were under."

I don't bother wasting time wondering how he knew about the fantastic sex I had with Zero. Probably smelled it on us after the crash or something. It doesn't matter.

"You don't deserve to lick the toilet she pisses in," I growl. I'm past caring about hiding it. Torture does loosen people's lips. When you're exhausted, with a world full of pain, it's hard to keep your mouth from talking. I lean into it while the torch hisses below every word I say. "She's gonna come here, fucking kill you by herself, and th—"

He applies the torch to the top of my thigh, and my vision flickers black and white. I let all my rage out, a bellowing roar that reaches to the ceiling and beyond, filling the room with my anger. The smell of burning slacks and skin compliment the torching of my skin. It's as if the devil himself has shoved his finger into my leg.

The spot of pain moves around my leg, down to my inner thigh, up to my groin. I'm out of breath but can't suck in more air to shout more. The room has gone almost black, vision tunneling down as resources are diverted to letting me know how much damage is being done.

When I'm almost to the point of passing into darkness, the hissing and crackling stops. My chin is down on my chest. The room is silent. The dark fog lifts from the center of my vision, and the sight of a charred line of skin, about the width of a quarter, is excruciating. There's no way to tell where the burning of my pants ends and my skin starts, because it's all fused together.

I summon the strength to lift my head, my gaze skipping over my shattered knees and mangled fingers, scanning the room around me. Costecu is gone, or at least isn't where I can see him.

"If you touch her, hurt her at all, I'll slice you into tiny pieces from the feet up," I croak out of my raw throat to the empty and stinking air. "It'll take weeks. Months."

If he's there, he doesn't reply. My head falls back down, and my eyes lose focus. He's left me to wallow in the thudding pain of my multiple injuries.

Using every reserve of energy I have, I channel it into the one limb that isn't injured, my right arm, tugging and yanking at the leather strap. Costecu's going to pay when I get out of here.

CHAPTER SEVEN

Aideen

My tub is large. It was one of the first things I changed from the original condo when I had the money. It's not a perfect circle, slight undulations making it seem more natural, like the curve of an ocean shore. There are jets all over, so many I've never counted, and they're controllable in different blocks. There are even a few lights for setting the proper mood, whatever I want it to be. I'm not sure what mood seaweed green is, but that's what I turn them to.

I crank the water full blast, more hot than cold. Next, I hit the button for the jets, all of them. It sounds like a waterfall, the rushing water noises echoing off the tile and mirrors like thunder.

I can't delay the pain any longer. With how beat up I am, this is going to hurt. I stand in front of my dressing mirror, to bolster courage, and start to peel off my clothes. I'm reminded they aren't my clothes as I unbutton the shirt with my right hand, my left arm and shoulder throbbing too much to consider moving.

Popping each button of Drew's shirt out with my thumb, wincing every time I forget and try to use my left arm, I reflect on how I got here, wearing the clothing of someone I know almost nothing about besides his criminal background. How each time he grabs me, I feel less anger and more desire. If anyone else had tried to manhandle me in the ways he has, I would've broken their fingers as a start.

Having gotten all the buttons undone, I grit my teeth and peel the fabric, soaked in dried blood, away from my skin and the bullet hole. It sticks and catches, sending little prickles of pain across my shoulder, which helps distract me from thinking about a man who's surely in pain to keep me safe.

"Ow, fuck, ow, fuck, ow, fuck," I mutter, watching the material come away from the skin. Red is smeared everywhere, a dull blotch across my skin. The last sticky part comes free, and I force my jaw to relax and slip my arm out. After that, it's simple to shrug my good arm out and let Drew's shirt flop to the floor, and with it the last vestiges of his subtle earthy scent I find I miss.

The pants are easier since they're way too big to begin with. Using my good arm gets the fly undone, though it's a bit odd to do it from the other side, and then I'm ready for my bath.

I take one last look in the mirror. Bedraggled, paler than normal, skin blotchy, and hair something you'd see on a barbarian. My stomach growls. Fuck I'm hungry. I'll need to eat soon.

I step in and I'm feeling all kinds of guilt. This bath is a luxury. Drew is out there getting tortured or worse because of his sacrifice to save me. I have to find a way to save him, as if that's going to be easy. Then, there's a dead body in my bedroom, and it would be a good idea to let my colleagues know I'm back and safe. That's if I have colleagues and a job.

I try to assuage my guilt by reminding myself I've been shot, and I can't wait to take care of that while trying to do what I should. I need a moment to myself, selfish as it is, to process, relax, and shed some of the mental pain as well as the physical. With this bath, I'll be better in thirty minutes. Thirty minutes of extra torture for Drew. Though I know he can take it and wouldn't trust anyone else to subject them to the same. It doesn't make me feel any less shitty about having jets of delicious water heal my body and soul.

I wonder what he does to chill. I've yet to see him hanging out. He's always on guard, even when he pretends to relax. When this is all over, I wonder if he's going to spend all that energy on me. The thought's enticing and intimidating.

The water is hot and soothing, and I can feel all the wounds I didn't know I had starting to heal. A cut in the middle of my back, a bruise on my calf, the ruined soles of my feet. I take a breath and slip under the water all the way, the jets pounding my exhausted muscles. The fire in my shoulder as the water takes hold hurts something fierce, and as my healing ability begins working as expected, it's unbelievably painful.

Regenerating skin and muscles push the bullet out. I pop my head back above the water to take long and deep breaths as the metal worms out the last agonizing inch. I bite back a curse as the skin stitches up, and snatch at the bullet rolling around the bottom of my tub. Flinging it in the general direction of my trash can, I'm rewarded with a satisfyingly metallic "tink."

The hard part over, I relax back in the seat, changing the jets direction to travel up and down my spine, along the underside of my thighs, and I rest my feet on a couple to get them pounded into submission. If it wasn't for the dead body of someone I thought was my friend in the other room, I could *almost* pretend everything is okay.

Resting my head against the padding, I close my eyes and let my worries take a back burner for a moment. It's like getting the best massage ever, a hundred hands kneading and hitting all at once. This tub was worth every expensive penny.

Images of Drew sneak into my mind: his piercing eyes, his neatly trimmed beard, and his voice, which holds confidence and command. The times he'd put himself in front of me when physical danger threatened. The way his hands had felt on my hips, my legs, and my back—the full and safe feeling when he'd been looming over me.

When we were joined there was nothing but me, him, and the urge overwhelming us. Any scrap of rationality I'd possessed told me he was dangerous and what we were doing was reckless. But logic left the building long before he held me. Distanced from our coupling by a day, logic still barely manages to make a half-hearted appearance.

It's not like me to fall for someone. My previous relationships have been slow and cautious like I conduct my life. I don't rush head-long into things in my job or personal life, which makes every interaction I've had with Drew an aberration. From the time I went into his cell alone, to the time I let him take me in his cabin. I danced at his speed, and I liked it...so much.

My fingers trail down my body. They're a poor substitute, but it's all I've got. My toy is in the bedroom, and if I go get it, I might come to my senses and stop. I don't want to stop fantasizing about Drew in all his reckless glory. A few satisfying but empty minutes later, I blow out the breath I'd been holding. Healed and full of determination aching to get stuff done, I have to get moving.

There are bad guys out there, one specifically who needs taking care of. Then I'll be able to relax for real. With any luck it won't be too late to save Drew.

Getting out of the heaven of my tub is difficult. The only thing that gets me moving is Drew. I can't deny the attraction between us, despite, or perhaps because of his controlling attitude. Leaving him to die isn't an option. He put everything on the line to get me safe, and I need to return the favor if for no other reason than I'm selfish. I'm nowhere near done with him.

I turn off the jets with a sigh and push myself out of the warm embrace of the soothing water. My wet feet slap across the floor as I walk to the closet to pull out some towels. Each fluffy scrub of the towel removes not only water but hesitation. I'm remembering who I am. I'm the person who was kidnapped and held against her will but didn't once give up. I'm capable of taking care of myself, and I'm capable of rescuing Drew.

I didn't get where I am by being helpless. I can handle stress and crisis with the best of them. I plan incursions, investigate terror and crime, and pull information from prisoners. People look up to me.

"You can fucking do this," I shout to myself in the mirror. I feel physically better. All the bruises and cuts are gone, and my hair is back to shiny and healthy. My skin glows, and not only from the healing water, but from resolve.

Filled back to my regular levels of confidence, I march out of the bathroom, past my bedroom, and into the living area. My work phone was last seen on the table outside the interrogation room days ago, but I keep an emergency backup in a kitchen drawer. The charging cable is wrapped around it, and the jack is taped to the back. Always prepared.

I plug it in, power it on, and wait for it to start up. I glance around, wrapping myself in the comfort of being at home, albeit with a dead person in my bedroom.

The kitchen is clean because I don't cook all that often. I work from home a lot but order out to save time. Still, there are good memories here of times when I'd get up early on a rare Saturday off and decide to make pancakes, bacon, and eggs. Or that one time I was determined to make my own noodles and bought a KitchenAid with attachments online. It still sits in the corner, a fun shade of green, unused.

The phone finishes updating and turns on with a beep. I check the time, try to remember who would be on shift this late, and dial the number for Safiya. She's an office peer, with the same responsibilities and almost the same authority, but works at night. The creatures we fight against are more active at night, so it's not the easy shift. She works hard.

Her assistant picks up the phone. "Miss Baha's office," she says, professional and crisp.

"Hey, it's me, Aideen. Is—"

The professional tone drops away, and she sounds like the young woman she is. "Oh my goodness, Miss Duffy. Are you okay? I've heard so many rumors. We've been so worried. Oh my gosh."

"Yes, Beth, I'm fine." She doesn't need to know about Jackson being dead, or me being shot, or anything else. It might make her head explode. "Is Safiya there?"

"Yes, hold on. I'll transfer you." I can imagine her quivering with gossip and unasked questions, but that's pixies for you. Always poking around in people's lives. Harmless, but annoying.

The phone clicks, there's a pause, and then Safiya picks up. "Aideen?"

"Hey. Yes, I'm all right," I say, heading off the obvious next question. "I'm going to need a clean-up crew. And I know where Costecu is located."

"Okay," she says. To her credit, there's no hesitation. She's always able to take on board the unexpected and adapt with an ease I wish I had. My strength is planning, hers is flexibility. "Where do you need the clean up?"

Right to business. Perfect. This is helping normalize everything. "My condo. It's Jackson."

"Is he hurt?" If she's surprised, her voice betrays nothing.

"No, he's dead. I killed him. He attacked me, Safi."

"Okay." She blows out a long breath. "It's going to be okay. I'll send over a crew ASAP, and I'll come over myself. You stay put. Are you okay?"

"Yes, I'm fine." I can feel her skepticism through the phone. "I had a bath, I'm not wounded anymore, it's fine. We've all been through this."

"Sure, but not in your own condo. That's...that has to be traumatizing. What do you mean wounded 'anymore'?"

"He shot me, but—"

"Okay, I'm coming over. You have any food? Eat something. Drink something. You're in shock, but it's going to wear off soon. I'll be there as soon as I can."

Sometimes her bossiness can get annoying, but right now it's nice to be told what to do. Plus, she's right. The bath helped with physical injuries, but at some point, it's all going to hit me mentally. "Okay."

"I'll see you in a few minutes. It's going to be all right." She hangs up, and I can imagine her dialing cleaning services. They're always on hand. Most cleaning they do is not of the kind you can schedule ahead of time. Then she'll storm out of her office, tell Beth to hold all her calls, and dial my boss to let him know what's going on.

Benjamin is a solid section lead. He stays out of my way and lets me do what's needed, even if it's occasionally not one hundred percent by the book. When I first transferred, I was put off by his gruff demeanor, but it turns out to be who he is, and not anything to do with me. I'm not sure what species he is, but he's old and from Bavaria somewhere. Perhaps with age came the ability not to micromanage.

My hand shakes as I put the cell back on the counter. I want and need to get dressed and out of these damp towels, but all my clothes are in the bedroom, so instead I open the fridge to see what's inside. Three-day old Ethiopian and older Vietnamese takeout. Various wilted vegetables, a product of wishful thinking, and some cheese I didn't wrap up tight that's a little fuzzy. I grab a cup of vanilla Greek yogurt I never got around to opening, along with a bottle of hard cider.

Inside the cabinet next to the fridge, I find some rolled oats. They go on top of the yogurt, and as I'm stirring them in and walking to the living room to sit on the couch, I pull up in a wash of memories.

The couch where Jackson was sitting, waiting for me, stares at me like an angry hobgoblin. I hesitate at the transition from tile to hardwood, standing next to the end of the cabinet. Dread seeps through me at the thought of sitting where he sat. I consider selling it, or maybe burning it. I'm sure I can't have it anywhere in my life from here on out.

I'm being dramatic. Drew wouldn't care. He'd walk over and sit on the couch and own it, take it back for himself. Hell, he'd probably sit on it with the dead body of someone he'd killed moments earlier draped over it still dripping blood. If we hadn't been found by Costecu, it's what I imagine him doing at his cabin. He killed those three people in his living room and wasn't bothered at all. He would've cleaned up the mess, lit a fire in the fireplace, and settled himself down to read a book with a glass of bourbon. Or maybe have more sex with me.

Setting my jaw and furrowing my brow, I march across the hardwood in my bare feet and plop into the middle of the couch. This is my fucking couch. I like this couch, and I'm not getting rid of it because one tiny bad thing happened. My. Fucking. Couch.

I eat the yogurt and oats with determination, ignoring the pit of fear trying to worm its way into my stomach, which seems to want solid food, and the yogurt isn't quite getting it. The alcohol starts to make me feel better.

I can do this. "I can do this," I say out loud. "This is easy shit. I'll finish this and then go into the bedroom and get dressed. It's not a big deal."

My voice sounds convincing, but I take smaller spoonfuls of yogurt the closer I get to being done. I can feel Jackson's body in there. An open and empty sore. A pit of red darkness. His angry eyes and menacing aura daring me to dislodge him.

Unbelievable, he's been working for Costecu all this time. We knew there was a mole, but it being him is unexpected. We'll need to launch an internal investigation to see what he compromised and if there are any more like him. Until then, I need to be careful. I'm not safe there. I know so much about Costecu and the operation. He'll be coming for me hard until I'm dead.

Someone knocks on my door, and I jerk to attention, wondering if it's another hitman. If Jackson —someone I considered stable and dependable—was hiding those thoughts, anyone could be.

I stare at the door harboring bucketloads of doubt. Is Safiya a double agent? She could be here to finish what Jackson started. I could've invited the enemy into my home.

Whoever it is knocks again. "Aideen? You in there?"

It is Safiya. I take a breath. She's fine, I tell myself. I'd notice. Right? Shit. I didn't notice Jackson.

"Aideen? Is everything okay? I'm coming in." She sounds determined.

I don't want her breaking down my door. "Wait. Sorry," I call out. "Hold on."

Padding back into the kitchen, I pull out my silverware drawer to grab the small gun I've got fastened underneath. The little entry hall seems to lengthen with every step I take, until I've got my hand on the lock. I click it over to open, take hold of the knob and turn, keeping my hand with the gun behind my back.

I peek out through the crack. "Safiya? Are you alone?"

She peers at me, forehead crinkled, her dark eyes searching my face. I get a glimpse of a crisp blazer and a wine-colored pencil skirt. "Yes. The cleaners won't be here for about thirty minutes. Why?"

"No reason," I mutter, scanning the hallway. Is that shadow moving? Further assailants might be hiding out of sight, ready to spring as soon as I open the door the rest of the way. I'm being ridiculous. She's not here to kill me. There's nothing in her heart-shaped face to indicate any deception. I open the door and step back to let her in. "Sorry. A little paranoid, I guess."

"Understandable," she says, sweeping past and brushing her black hair over her shoulders. She walks into the living area, leaving me to close and lock the door behind her. "Where's the body?"

"In my bedroom."

She glances at me after her quick survey of the room. "Explains why you're still in towels. You don't look so good. Are you hiding something behind your back?"

My shoulders slump as I drop my hand to reveal the gun. "Maybe more than a little paranoid."

Then everything hits me all at once, from beginning to end. Drew's interrogation. How my negligence let him out, the horrible time when I thought he was my enemy, facing down Costecu, being tortured, my escape and flight to the cabin, the worry, watching Drew kill that huge dragon, the sex, the crash, the journey home, killing Jackson.

Everything goes blurry and the gun falls from my fingers, rattling on the hardwood. It's good I didn't turn the safety off.

In a moment Safiya is there, pulling me to the couch, sitting down next to me, and I can't stop the tears.

CHAPTER EIGHT

Druain

I've been staring at the dark brown leather strap binding my right wrist for what feels like hours while I strain, trying anything to gain a bit of freedom. I've managed to get perhaps a centimeter of give so far. I can slide my arm back and forth a fraction of an inch. Give me another week or so and I'll be out of here.

My knees are still shattered since I can't move them to get the extra blood flow I'd need to speed up the process. Costecu left the needles under my fingernails, but since he also broke the fingers, I don't really notice the needles.

"This place isn't getting a good review," I mutter.

Talking out loud helps me maintain sanity, as long as I don't reveal anything. No one's watching me. After Costecu left, some former colleagues came around to gloat, but it was easy to ignore them. None came in the room, instead jeering at me through the barred window, so Costecu must have been clear I wasn't to be touched. He wants me all to himself.

He's out there, free as a bat, trying to track down Zero with no one to stop him. I have to get out of here right fucking now or him finding her will be all my fault.

I glare at the strap again. I've figured out it's been bolted directly to the petrified wood of the chair, which is why I can't get it to budge. There's no buckle or clasp to break, no weak spot to exploit. They bound me in here with no expectation I'll ever leave, short of cutting the leather off.

I've tried rocking some more, but the concrete isn't going to give up the legs, and the wood is far too hard to snap. I can't lean down to check, but I'm sure the leather holding my ankles is also bolted. I can't move my legs much anyway on account of the exploding pain from my knees.

The only hope is my right hand, the one he didn't destroy, so that's what I've been working on. I'll get there.

Someone else comes to peer at me through the bars, and this time I change focus from my escape attempt. Maybe I can use them in some way. People are a lot weaker than inanimate objects.

"Look what we have here," he says, a smirk on his face.

I have no idea who he is. Some juvenile vamp. Probably thinks he's the shit. "Who are you?" I ask, making sure to furrow my brow. That ought to piss him off. Maybe if I can get him to come inside, I can...do something. I'm sure I'll figure out the next step of this plan at some point.

"Who am...seriously? You don't remember me?"

That was easy. I'd expected to have to bait him more. "Sorry, no. I've slept with a lot of people."

His eyes shoot open before he grabs the bars and shoves his face as close as he can. "We didn't sleep together, you pervert. I sleep with women."

"Cool. Good for you. Me too, but I didn't want to assume, you know? It's a good idea to be inclusive. There've been a few times, you know, had a lot to drink..."

"Shut up, you fucker."

I have no idea what I did to this guy, but it must've been something impressive. He's got a short fuse, zero common sense, and all the sensitivity of a brick. "I kinda can't do anything but talk, so I'll keep going if that's okay with you. Being strapped to this chair and everything. Thanks for stopping by, I was getting bored."

"Shut up."

"So what do you want to talk about?"

"I don't want to talk about anything." His face is bright red. What a chump.

"Oh. Then why are you here?"

He growls, an actual teeth-baring growl, fangs and all. Maybe I can tempt him to bite me, bringing him in range. "I came to see the all high and mighty dwarf bootlicker all locked up."

I gesture the best I can with my head, which was a mistake to leave free. "Welp, here I am. Is it exciting? I kind of feel like I might be a letdown. Probably not bleeding enough, don't you think?" I wiggle my broken fingers, which hurts like a bitch, but might pop a scab or something.

His nostrils flare as I get some bleeding to start. "You really don't remember me?" he asks, stuck between rage and confusion.

"Nope. Sorry. There's a whole lot of you idiots, and I didn't need to know names to keep you all under control. You guys aren't that smart."

He sucks in a breath through his teeth, grimacing in anger, before smacking the bars a few times with his hand. "You almost killed me, you bastard, and you don't remember?"

"I've killed way more people than I've slept with, and I don't remember any of them either, so the odds of me remembering someone I *didn't* kill are slim." I give him a slow up and down scan. "Plus, you don't look all that special. I probably wouldn't remember you even if I'd fucked you and then killed you."

His rage goes incandescent. For a species that's supposed to be intelligent, vampires are pretty easy to manipulate. They're vain, believing the whole world revolves around them, and when anyone admits they don't know or care the slightest, they tend to go volcanic.

"Not that I'd do either," I continue. "You aren't my type, and you aren't important enough to kill. Some human will probably accidentally off you in some hilarious way, like beheading you with a circular saw."

With a shriek that could only be described as eldritch, he tears away from the bars and starts bashing himself against the other side of the door. Costecu must have locked it. A normal lock wouldn't last five seconds, but we don't use normal locks around here. The door is somewhat reinforced, but he still manages to make a dent on the other side.

"Having some trouble?" I call out. "I'd help, but, well...you know."

Another screech and another series of metallic clangs, and then he bursts back into view on the other side of the viewing bars. "Fuck you."

"I honestly thought you'd be able to get in," I state. "Costecu must not want anyone messing with me. Better do what the boss wants. Scurry along now."

"I'll be back," he snarls, then disappears in the other direction.

"That's kind of cliche," I shout after him.

It's not difficult for me to assume he's off to get some reinforcements to come and try again. I spend the time working on my wrist strap, as I've been doing the whole time, and wondering what I did to him. The way he reacted, I kind of wish I remembered. It must've been marvelous.

It comes to me after a few minutes of wracking my brain. It had been about a year ago. He was a new vampire back then, fresh off of a turning and hopped up on ego and the power of live blood. I'd taken him along on what I called a fishing mission.

There had been rumors a minotaur had moved into town, and I'd been tasked to find out if it was true, and if so get him to join us, or kill him if he refused. It turned out the rumors were true, and I tracked him down pretty easily. As careful as minotaurs tend to be, it's hard to hide when they're as large as I am and prone to road rage. Something about stop lights sets them off.

I'd found where he'd lived, and was judging how to approach, watching him for a few days. This young punk, who had been pissing me off for a week because he kept trying to pick fights and wouldn't settle down, ran across my path, so I snagged him to go out on the last day of observation. Figured I'd teach him a lesson or two about respect.

Then, when we were sitting outside the minotaur's house in our SUV, I'd told the vamp the guy was making life hard for us, and I wanted him to go take him out. The idiot sprang out of the SUV, tore up the front steps, and shattered the door on the way inside.

I figured, best case scenario I'd be out a worthless vamp who couldn't keep his proverbial dick in his pants, and worst case I'd have to beat him myself for harming a potential asset.

The minotaur sent him flying back out of the door with two broken legs and a smashed jaw, but nothing else to my disappointment. I had the minotaur recruited ten minutes later. As much as I wanted to leave the vamp there to crawl back, I couldn't risk him being in the open, so I'd tossed him in the back seat and drove to base, forgetting about him long before I parked. I guess he managed to get out of the SUV and found a blood bag to heal.

Good times.

He returns with friends, as expected. A motley crew of angular faces pass by the window, four of them, all glaring at me with death in their eyes. They're not wrong there.

As the last one disappears and the banging on the metal door starts, much louder than last time, I reach a decision.

Gritting my teeth, glad that Costecu didn't start with them, I concentrate every bit of strength I have left. The tiny space between the leather strap and the wood isn't enough for my hand to fit through without breaking or dislocating my thumb. I'd been trying to avoid that outcome, to keep one part of me unbroken, but my time is up.

I time the snap to the rhythm of the banging on the door, and my hand slips free of the bond. My elbow slams against the back of the chair. That bit of unexpected pain is worse than the expected one of having a broken thumb.

"Ow," I mutter. Perfect. I've got one hand free, minus the use of my broken thumb. My other hand is shattered, my knees are useless, and I still can't move from where I'm bound, yet I'm ready to take on these vamps and get out of here.

The lock gives way, and the door topples inside on one hinge, creaking and groaning as the metal twists and it falls to the floor.

"Hi guys," I greet the four glowering faces, keeping my freed hand in position. They're too idiotic to notice it's not restrained. "Did Costecu send you to help me out? What a guy, am I right?"

They share a couple furtive glances, perhaps aware that they'll get in serious trouble if found out, but the leader growls and steps forward. "You're going to pay."

"Do you take debit?"

He howls and lunges forward, like an idiot, and while he's faster than a human, he's still nowhere near the speed of Costecu or a vampire with a couple of decades on him.

I grab him around the neck, my broken thumb screaming in pain as the muscles force the bones to hold together, but he still crashes into me from the momentum of his charge. He makes a strangled sound of surprise as I lift him off of me with my one arm, his hands gripping my arm, his instinct to pull me off.

"I'm not going to remember you this time, either," I tell him while his friends watch from the doorway. I glance over at them. "Looks like your friends aren't your friends after all. I'd give you some advice on how to actually gain loyalty, but I think it's too late."

The rest of the interlopers stare as the vamp's face turns purple then blue, while he thrashes at the end of my arm. His feet are planted on the floor, but I'm crushing his windpipe. It won't kill him permanently, but what I'll do after he's knocked out sure will.

"You guys and gals will have to wait your turn."

They turn as one and run away. The vamp gurgles one more time as his eyes roll back in his head and he goes limp.

"Damned idiots," I mumble to myself, pushing him to the floor in a heap. I poke around my pocket for the knife that's been digging into my hip this whole time. Costecu is so arrogant he didn't bother to search me. How this operation is still running is beyond me.

I pull it out and am reminded of Zero. It's the same knife I made her use to cut the tracker out of her hip. That soft and delicate patch of skin is still the most erotic thing I've ever seen, even counting seeing her totally naked and being buried inside her.

It seems *that* part of me is still working. If I somehow lose my legs from this, which I won't, I'll still be able to have sex with her. A whole lot of sex.

My thumb shoots pain up my wrist as I flick the blade open and get to sawing at the strap holding down my left wrist. I study the smashed fingers without much emotion. I've seen mangled fingers before, done it to people a few times, broken my own a couple. It's no big deal. Part of my life.

The leather is old but supple, good quality, but the knife wins in the end, and I drag my hand out. My fingers dangle like wet noodles. I pull the needles out with a sharp zing of heat from each one running up my wrist and forearm.

Then I bend over to cut my ankles free. Costecu left my shoes on, another mistake. I take delight in knowing I've got him so off-balance. Pissing people off is pretty much my hobby, always has been, and I guess I'm lucky I have a job where I can do it all the time.

I'm not sure to where in the real world the skill will translate over when all this is over, but I'm sure some company will hire me to yell at people. I've never allowed myself to waste time wondering what my life would be if I got out of this. All of my adult life has been taken up getting where I am with a singular focus. Once it's over, I won't have anywhere to go or anything to do. Maybe I'll get a dog.

Both feet are free. I'll just have to stand up, with my broken knees, and all the old injuries from yesterday, and walk on out of here. Easy.

I brace on the arm of the chair with my nominally good hand, and lever myself up. My knees crack and shift, I wobble and groan as inch by inch I push myself upright. It's excruciating. Top ten for sure. I haven't had to move so much so soon after a major injury in a while. Most times I get to rest first, let some of the smaller wounds heal before tackling the larger ones.

Tottering over to the wall to support myself better, I take some breaths. Knees need to be worked on first, so I can walk and then run, while my hands can be left for later. My broken thumb is throbbing, but at least it's functional.

As before, I start to pace, one foot in front of another, getting the blood flowing. Flowing blood means healing bones and stronger muscles. I don't have all the time in the world, so I need to get going, but if I leave too early, I won't be able to defend myself. It's a judgment call, but I make great judgment calls.

I knew Zero was amazing as soon as I clapped eyes on her, and I was correct.

Each step drives spikes through my knees, but I keep going. Around and around the room. Every minute also makes me more restless. Costecu could be back any moment. Zero could be in danger, and here I am, hobbling like an old man, all because someone tapped my knees a little.

That pushes me out of the room and down the hallway. It hurts, but I ignore the pain. It's all in the mind, telling me I'm injured, but I can ignore it, and keep ignoring it as long as needed.

Voices are echoing along the hallways. There must be something going on from the prison break I facilitated. Wouldn't be surprised. That much chaos would've left everyone scurrying around, distrustful, and disorganized.

With Costecu brooding over me, I suspect he hasn't given much direction, and since I was the one who kept everything under control, there's a power vacuum. Maybe they're all killing each other, which would be swell.

I'm so caught up in imagining the destruction and mayhem racing around this place I don't notice Costecu until I'm within five feet of him. Then again, he might have been following me this whole time, and I wouldn't've noticed. He's so quiet.

"Oh. Hey. Just stretching my legs," I say, refusing to give into the anger and disappointment.

"I'm disappointed in you," he says, as if I should be ashamed.

"Yeah. Me too. I should be crushing your skull, but I can't move too well. Can't imagine why."

"I see I'm going to have to resort to other measures to get you under control."

My casual attitude drops away like metal shutters, revealing the hard core of my determination. "You'll never control me," I spit with every ounce of conviction I possess.

"Yes, I will."

I don't see him move until he's right in my face, and then things go black again.

CHAPTER NINE

Aideen

I pull myself back together. It's not doing any good to sit and snivel on my couch. Drew would give me a scathing glare if he saw me acting like this. In that last moment before I got away from the crash, he told me to rescue him, and that's what I'm going to do. I would've done it even if he hadn't said a single word. I can't leave someone behind.

"I'm fine. Thanks. I'm okay," I say, letting go of Safiya and wiping my eyes. "Just tired."

"How long has it been since you've slept?"

I have to think about it for a second. "I guess, I mean it hasn't actually been that long. It's only midnight? It feels like a lot more. After eight hours of walking through the woods, and...and then this..." I wave my arm in the general direction of my bedroom where Jackson's body still is.

"Sounds horrible, but you can tell me later, okay?" She pats my knee and then stands up. "Let me go check it out and I'll get you some clothes, okay? Do you need anything from the kitchen?"

"No. It's fine. Thanks." I wave her away.

She flashes one of those tight smiles you give to people in distress and moves off down the hall. I lean back against the couch, blowing out a long breath. So much has happened in the past eighteen hours. My muscles are still aching, but it might be tension from not knowing what's going on with Drew.

A few minutes later Safiya comes back, carrying a pair of yoga pants and a loose top. "I wasn't sure what you wanted, so I went for something comfortable."

"Perfect, thanks." I fight down my irrational irritation at her rhetorical statements, meant to soften the blow of commands. It's a habit of hers I hate.

She turns her back as I shed the towels and slip on the clothes. "Is it as bad as I remember?" I ask, pulling the top down and freeing my hair.

"You're probably going to want a whole new mattress and sheets, I'll say that. Carpet too."

"Ugh. I'm dressed. We need to talk real quick before the cleaners get here." I sit back down on the couch.

"Yeah? What's going on?"

She needs to know Drew helped me, that he's turned and is working against Costecu. I'm not going to tell her he's one of ours. I'm don't trust her that much. I am going to make clear he's someone we need to extract, protect, and use to our advantage. "You remember Druain Lindberg? Costecu's right-hand man."

"Of course. You captured him the other day, and he broke out and took you with him." She folds her hands in her lap.

"Oh, yeah." It seems so long ago, and so surreal, I can't believe it all happened. "Well, he's the reason I got out. He helped me. I think he's on our side." She chews her lip and won't meet my eyes. "Safi? What's going on?"

"Yeah, sorry. I already knew, He's been deep undercover for over a year, and I've been his handler."

"What?" I sit back.

"Sorry, Aideen. I wanted to tell you, but..."

"More than a year?"

"Command wanted to make sure there was as little risk as possible of getting him exposed."

"They couldn't tell *me*?" The hot burn of anger settles in my chest. All this time, and I could have been using him, communicating my needs, coordinating strikes.

"We've been working off of his info all this time."

"I could have...they...that would have helped me so much."

"I shared everything relevant he gave me," she says. "We coordinated with your operation as much as possible without exposing him."

"I could have coordinated better. It's my operation. I needed to know he was there." I shouldn't be upset at her, but she's a convenient target. I'm bone-deep exhausted, and I can't help but feel betrayed.

"I'm sorry, Aideen. They were worried you'd be too close to the situation. You know the protocols."

I helped re-write the protocols when I came onboard because they were primitive and left too much to good intentions and guesswork. Inside assets should always be handled by someone other than the agent in charge of the overarching operation. "Yes, of course I know the protocols. Sorry. Sorry, I'm...sorry." I massage my temples.

"It's okay." She sits, calm and straight-backed while I work out my frustrations.

"I...this could have helped so much. I get it, obviously, I get it. Obviously. It would've been good to know."

"So he broke character?" She's changing the subject, trying to get me to the important part, and I'm too tired to protest.

"I guess. Yeah." I rub my forehead. I'm not going to tell her everything, for obvious reasons. I'll stick with the most important parts. "In the most disruptive way. Long story, but we ended up at a cabin he has in the woods, which is where Costecu found us. Lindberg got nabbed, and I managed to get back here. His cover is blown." I can't very well call him Drew in front of her. Talk about giving too much away.

Safiya bumps a fist on her thigh. "Damn it. That's a lot of time wasted."

"Not really. Now I know where Costecu is based. We can get a team together, extract Lindberg, and shut Costecu down for good."

"You want to go in with force?" She leans back, crosses her arms, and peers at the ceiling. "There's going to be a lot of people there. It'll be a bloodbath."

"We'll have the element of surprise," I say, putting my elbows on my knees and staring at the hardwood floor. "Yes, it'll be dangerous, but we can end this once and for all. Wipe out Costecu, and strays and independent psychos from here on out." Discounting all the other cities, with all our other branches, all fighting the same fight as me.

"Will we? Costecu knows you're out. He'll be expecting us."

"Not yet. That's why Jackson was here. He was supposed to kill me."

She doesn't seem convinced, twisting her lip down and scratching her chin. "I don't know."

"This is definitely the time. Before Costecu figures out Jackson failed."

Before I can make any further arguments to get her on my side or pull rank and take the correct course of action direct to the board to get approval, there's a knock on the door. The cleaners no doubt.

She moves to get up, but I do first. "I'll get it. I'm fine." It's true. Thinking about getting out and rescuing Drew has given me energy, not to mention ending Costecu's blight. The former is more important than the latter, but I won't be admitting that.

I check the spyhole, then open the door for the cleaning crew. Four people, carrying all sorts of large bags of equipment. "We understand you've got a situation."

"Yes. In the bedroom. Thank you." I let them in and plop onto the couch, watching them set up in the hallway. Zippers and rustling of bags follow as they change into those plastic-y white sterile uniforms. If they have any thoughts about what they see, they keep it to themselves like the professionals they are.

I don't want to talk anymore. I'm a bit stressed out by strangers in my condo and content to apply my brainpower to the coming rescue. Safiya stays silent as well, and we both watch as one goes out and comes back hauling more equipment. At least it's the middle of the night, and most people will be asleep, so they won't be wondering what happened.

The industrial vacuum is loud, which is *not* great at night, but I didn't buy a cheap condo. The walls should insulate against most of the noise. The sound is almost meditative, a constant drone pushing out all thought, emptying my brain of worries. The need to do something right this instant becomes paramount.

Drew could be dead. He could be strapped to a chair like I was, with his fingernails being pulled out. He could be hung from the ceiling with his entrails being pulled out inch by inch. I need to get him back. I won't let him die after everything he did.

My eyes are heavy, and even with the noise and people in my condo, I could fall asleep. Sleep is a luxury Lindberg can't afford, so I keep rubbing and pinching my face to stay awake.

Safiya eyes me. "You need a nap?" she shouts over the machines.

I shake my head. Not going to succumb. There are things to do, and I want to do them. I want everyone to leave so I can think and get ready for how I'm going to convince everyone to raid Costecu's lair.

At one point the engine tone changes. It must not be only the vacuum anymore, but I'm not sure what else they use. The machines turn off, and the cleaners start to carry out all sorts of bags, sealed tight and lumpy. They're winding down.

One comes up to me, pulling her mask up and plastic safety goggles off, the clean white of their suits spattered with dark red and other disturbing colors.

"We're about done, ma'am. We had to take up the carpet, and we trashed all your bedding. We'll be taking the bed out shortly, and then we'll be done."

"The whole bed?"

"Yup. The mattress is kind of obvious, but you can keep the frame if you want. The wood is a bit stained, probably won't get it all clean. I'd recommend you get rid of it though, and not only because of the stain." Her expression is set with the experience of one who has seen many horrible things.

"Fine," I sigh in resignation. The company will pay in part for replacing things, so it's not worth risking the potential mental effects of sleeping in a bed frame someone died on. Not having to pay thousands of dollars for a specialized cleaning company is a nice bonus. "Take all of it."

They haul the mattress out, the side with the stain facing away from me. The urge to get up and help so I'm doing something is strong, but I'd be getting in their way. They're professionals, it's their job, and I don't want to be that type of person. It would piss me off to no end if some random, untrained person tried to help me do my job.

"That's it, ma'am. Let us know if you need anything else."

"Thanks."

They leave and shut the door behind them, and I'm up and walking into the bedroom before Safiya can stop me. "I guess I always wanted hardwood in my bedroom anyway," I say, studying what's left. Whoever owned the condo last covered up some really intricate wood flooring. It'll need to be cleaned and resealed, but I could live with it like it is.

"It doesn't look too bad," Safiya says behind me, peeking over my shoulder. "Why didn't you have it redone?"

I shrug. "Never really had the time. Didn't get around to it."

The room feels so much bigger without my bed in it, and I toss around several ideas for rearranging in my head, but then put them aside. I'm trying to distract myself from what comes next, while part of me is begging to take a break. "I need to go into the office and plan. We're going in."

She raises an eyebrow. "You need to sleep. You can figure out what you want to do tomorrow?"

"Not a chance," I say, marching over to my closet to start sorting through clothes. "Things have to get done. If you want to help, brew me up some coffee. The bag is in the upper cabinet right above the sink."

She sighs and walks off to the kitchen. I've gone a few days without sleep before, and I can do it again. I got plenty of sleep at the cabin. About ten minutes later I smell instant coffee, and five minutes after that I'm dressed in slacks and a blouse, standing at the mirror in my bathroom to throw on some makeup.

"Thank you," I call out, finishing the mascara.

"I'm doing this under protest," she says, walking in and setting a mug down on the counter.

I grab at it and suck down half of it at once. The warmth sliding down my throat and resting in my stomach is much appreciated. "Oh, yeah. That's it. I mean, it's instant, so it's gross, but it's still good. The cafe at work is so much better."

"Spoiled day-timer," she says with a slight grin.

"Huh?"

"You know it's not open at night. We have to make our own."

"That's one thing I'm not jealous of. That, and the weird hours."

She crosses her arms and leans against the door frame. "Are you sure I can't convince you to sleep?"

"Nope. You know me."

"Unfortunately. You work way too late, way too often."

I step back from the mirror and carry my mug with me into the kitchen. "Someone's gotta do it."

"There are other people, you know. We all work together," she says, following me.

"I know. You know what I mean, but I can't do nothing. Tell me about Lindberg." I grab my travel mug from the dishwasher, fill it with coffee, snag my spare phone, and reach for keys that aren't there. They're in my drawer, in my desk, in my office. "Shit. My car's still at work. Can I get a ride?"

"Of course. You lost your phone?"

"I had it when I... When Lindberg broke out. I hope it's still on the table or someone returned it to my desk."

"We'll check when we get there. There were people combing over the room trying to figure how he got out, so they probably put it in evidence. How did he get out?"

"Uh, I guess the door was weak or something." I might have to tell the truth at some point, but this isn't that time, and she's not the person I want to have that information. "He burst through it when I was in the other room and grabbed me."

She makes a noise but doesn't say anything else. There's no way she knows. We don't keep cameras down there for security purposes. We can't have someone hacking in and seeing who we're interrogating. Plus, some creatures react badly to being recorded, either in person or when trying to watch it back.

Her car is parked in my spot in the garage, and a short drive later it's parked in the garage in the office building where we have our offices. A ride up the elevator and I'm back. It feels more like home than my actual home, which isn't surprising since I spend most of my time here.

The doors to the elevator open with a ding, and Frank is there waiting to greet me. He grabs me up in an unexpected hug, his white hair tickling under my chin.

"You're safe. Thank the lord. I was so worried about you."

"Ughf," I grunt. "What are you doing here? It's past midnight."

"Miss Baha texted me all about it. I had to be here when you got in. You poor thing."

I turn to raise an eyebrow at her. She shrugs. "He was sick with worry the whole time you were gone."

"Fine." I return my attention to Frank. "Gather up everything I've got on Druain Lindberg. I need to know full history, from when we first found out about him to all of the reports about the last couple of days. I need to create a flashy bio the board can digest."

"Right away," he says, dashing off as fast as he can, without one question. That's what I like about him. Doesn't waste my time trying to understand every little thing, or badger me with questions. He does his job and does it well.

"First," Safiya says, grabbing my arm as I'm about to head to my office. "We need to get you debriefed."

"Oh, come on Safi," I protest, itching to get started on something constructive and actionable. Something to work on getting Drew back. "I'd like to set some things in motion."

"No. You know the rules? We need to get it down while it's still fresh."

I roll my eyes. "Yes, I know the regulations, but—"

"No 'buts.' Debrief. Now."

"Ugh."

"We're going to get every single thing down. They're going to want to know before they decide what to do."

"I've already decided what to do," I mutter, but follow after her to one the conference rooms, trying to figure out how I'm going to tell the story while leaving out the parts no one needs to know.

CHAPTER TEN

Druain

I wake up strapped to a chair again. On closer inspection I find it's the same chair, with new straps. Also, more straps and my hands are nailed to the wood. Same room, too, judging by the light and the same old torture instruments.

"I'd like a new room, please," I say without preamble. Costecu is here somewhere.

"I don't think you understand the gravity of the situation you're in."

"I'm in a situation?"

"A dire one, in fact. For you." He walks around from behind me. He likes that kind of reveal. It's stylish.

"I've been in worse." The top of the nails are clean and shiny, not rusty, so that's a plus. I won't get tetanus. It still hurts like hell. I attempt a foot wiggle, sending my knees into sparks, and find them free. I start working my right foot. If I can get it out, maybe I can get into my pocket, grab the knife with my toes...

"I can hear you move, hear your broken bones trying to reform," he tells me, as if imparting great wisdom. His chin is tilted up and he's pacing back and forth across the room in slow and measured steps. I feel like I'm in the most macabre lecture hall ever, with a teacher who doesn't want his students leaving early when he gets to the boring parts. Hence the restraints. "I know you're in no condition to do anything."

"You didn't secure my feet," I respond, tossing out a random fact.

"There will be no need. The nails in your hands," he gestures to said nails. "Are only for effect. To let you know there are consequences to your actions. You won't be here long enough to escape. A mere fifteen to thirty minutes, perhaps."

"That's good, because, honestly, the ambiance here stinks."

"You can also rest assured that the ones who enabled your escape are being severely punished. I expect them to be alive for at least another week."

"Sounds like a win-win. You get to act on your murderous and primitive desires, and the world is freed of four more bloodsuckers. You have no idea how many of your own people you've taken out. We wouldn't need to be constantly recruiting if you could keep your teeth in your pants."

"Cut out the weak, and those remaining become strong."

I nod in mock agreement. "You're going to be like Superman then, when everyone else is dead."

"Enough of this pathetic wordplay," he spins to face me and lowers his gaze to mine. "Is there anything you'd like to confess before I hollow you out into shell for me to control?"

I raise my eyes to the ceiling in thought. "Hmm. I'm really not that fond of coffee. You'd think, being a dwarf, I'd be all over the bitter stuff, but nope. Prefer a good glass of orange juice. Healthier, too."

He stomps out of the room in a subtle temper-tantrum, although it might be my imagination. He crosses in front of the bars, a dim figure with a slight roll to his shoulders and a long nose. I'm reminded of that old movie, *Nosferatu*, and the way the monster cast his shadow against the wall.

My right leg isn't making much progress. This might take a bit longer than before, and the ankle would be harder to break than the thumb on my hand.

The good news is he's still here in his lair and not out looking for Zero. I blunt the pain from my hands and fingers and knees by thinking about her. Her skin was so soft every time I'd grabbed her, which is one reason why I did it so much. Does she use expensive body soap, or is it a selkie thing? When I get out of here, I'm going to spend a full day touching every single inch of her body and doing nothing else.

The ways her eyes sparked in anger and defiance at every barb I threw her way is something I enjoy way too much. She didn't once cower or seem hurt by it, speaking to her strong sense of self. She's confident, that's for sure, and I love that. How anyone could like a woman who's so demure and emotionally squishy, I don't know. I need someone who can take as much as they give.

My right knee is feeling better. On the scale from thermite burns to fireworks, it's around a shrapnel grenade.

Her breasts are fantastic. I figured they would be from the moment I saw her in that boring white blouse. As non-form-fitting as it was, it was clear she was hiding a great pair behind the boring business attire. I was pretty proud of myself how I restrained I was from finding an excuse to rip it off in the SUV.

Then when she came out of the shower with a simple towel wrapped around her fucking perfect body. I almost lost it. It'd taken everything I had to turn from the door she was trying to hide behind, her fresh scent wafting from out of the small gap, the slight crack in her voice telling me everything I dreamed of.

That instant when I'd ripped the towel off her, exposing her to my hungry eyes, pushed her down, watched how her chest moved with every excited breath, the manicured patch between her legs wet for me, I could have come all over her in that second, but that wouldn't have been a polite thing to do on the first date.

I grunt. If only they'd bound me here by my dick, I'd be free.

Noise outside the cell interrupts my fond memories and plans for the future. It can't be Costecu. I wouldn't hear him at all, except then he glides into view. I'm saved from wondering what the sighing sound accompanying him is. The wet weeping is a damn banshee who floats across my vision.

Banshees, like dragons, are rare. I've never met one, seen one, or gotten anywhere close to one. They tend to destroy people in their vicinity with their constant psychic attacks, rooted in pain and loss. Most of them can't control what they do any more than I could control my bones knitting back together.

Like most human stories, the myths about banshees have a kernel of truth to them. They don't wail for the dead, instead the dead are the ones they're wailing at. From what I understand, their voice gets in your brain somehow, like a siren song, and you relive all sorts of horrible memories.

Each one strips away a part of your mind as the banshee eats your guilt and pain. At some point you snap, driven to the edge by the psychic torture, and then she siphons the last of your will, leaving you as an empty shell, mind destroyed, a vessel to be commanded until death.

I can't let that happen.

I wipe my face clean of emotions, but there's no stopping the involuntary body response. My heart rate shoots up, faster than ever, and I'm sure I start emitting fear pheromones Costecu will pick up on.

He opens the door with a self-satisfied smile, holding a leash attached to the body harness the banshee is in. Her face is bound in a mask with only her red-rimmed eyes showing through like brake lights on a foggy night.

"Ah, I can hear by your pulse you finally understand," Costecu says. "I'd give you a chance to cooperate willingly, but I'm afraid I'm rather set on this course of action."

I'd like to ask him where he found a banshee, and where he's been keeping her, and if he's out of his damn mind, but it would give him too much satisfaction. It doesn't matter at this point anyway. No reason to be curious about things that won't help the situation. He could tell me he birthed her himself, and it wouldn't change what I need to do.

I close my eyes so I can't see her face, and start to build walls in my mind. If the rumors are true, and I have no reason to take them as anything but, things are about to get ugly.

"Yes, well, I can see you're taking this seriously, so I'll leave you two to get acquainted." He chuckles in that damn dry paper shuffling that makes me want to burn out his lungs.

I keep my eyes closed tight and try not to get distracted by a tiny sound of metal on metal, the sound of the door opening then closing, the metal shutter being lowered over the bars, putting the room in isolation.

I try not to listen to the weeping and moaning itching at the corner of my brain, and getting a tiny bit louder every second.

It's hard to ignore. The itching turns to persistent scratching, worming through my thoughts like a trail of gasoline waiting for the match. I've never trained for this sort of thing, always focusing on physical intimidation and letting my mental exercises go undone. I'd never expected to need them, not to this degree. Banshees aren't supposed to be around anymore, at least not in any state where they'd be capturable. Get within a quarter mile of one and you should be writhing on the ground, sucking your thumb and bawling like a baby.

Costecu must have gotten her himself. He's old enough to have a mind of steel, and being a vampire doesn't hurt. He could approach a weaker one and come out okay. Damn it. Why didn't I plan for this? I should've known he'd have something in his back pocket. I underestimated him.

The wailing is on the low threshold of human hearing, a keening cutting like a knife. The muzzle must be starting to melt away under the psychic assault.

The knowledge she's going to overcome me sits heavy in my mind. It's pointless to try to fight, it's just going to hurt more.

Fuck, I'm already doubting myself. That's not a good sign. I move my feet, my hands, gnaw on my lip, wiggle my fingers, anything to cause myself pain. Sharp pain, something glimmering and bright I can hold on to.

Pack shit away. Remember the important things. Find something to keep.

There's a sizzling noise under the keening. By the horrible smell, it's the leather mask being melted. A pinging noise might be one of the metal rivets holding it together hitting the floor.

The fire licking at my memories and control is growing. My mind is doused in accelerant, black tar, needles, and the hungry flame weaves through everything, the knowledge that everyone ends, everyone dies. Nothing lasts forever. It would be easier to give up than fight in the darkness, alone.

No. I'm not alone. Zero is coming. She will. She's not going to leave me in this pit, not after everything we've gone through. I saw the way she looked at me. I saw the need. The longing, the heat as I entered her. The pure pleasure as she came.

It's gone. She's gone because I was careless and let Costecu find us. She made it into the woods, only to break her ankle in a hole. She's still out there, crawling, hungry, thirsty, miles from home, the buzzards overhead, the wolves on her trail.

Fuck. There aren't any buzzards here. She's fine. She's smart. She made it home. She's tough, alive, and she's getting every gun they've got and is going to arrive any second. That screaming isn't me, it's the sound of anyone who would oppose her.

She's dead. My parents are dead, my siblings are dead. They're all dead, and it's because of me. I killed them, as surely as if I'd pulled the trigger myself.

No, I didn't kill my family. That's not what happened.

I let them get killed. I ran away, I let them get killed. I knew what would happen. Costecu killed them. I knew he would, and I let him. I wanted him to kill them.

I didn't know a fucking thing. I didn't know he was there. I didn't know what they were involved in. I didn't know my parents had refused to work with him. My brother, my sister...they didn't know anything.

I should've stayed. I should've fought. I could've changed everything. They'd still be alive if I'd been there, if I could've fought Costecu. They're dead, just like Zero is dead.

I let them die.

Zero's not dead.

The keening rockets up into a screech. Unfiltered, driving spikes into my eardrums. The note isn't from the earth at all, but somewhere deep and dark. A place where the hottest bonfire would freeze in an instant. My face is wet. Tears, snot, blood.

Everyone's going to die. We're all going to be wiped out, one by one, picked off and cut to ribbons. The darkness is going to win. The darkness will win. Everyone will be snuffed out. I'm already dead. Your family is dead. Zero is dead.

Zero isn't dead. Zero is alive. She's alive. Alive.

Everyone is dead.

I open my eyes. The banshee is quiet. Her face is pure sadness. She's weeping, tears running down well-worn tracks in her face, channels of pain and sorrow. She closes her mouth, but for a small moment of time I can see the black stubs and jagged edges of her teeth. Her tongue is purple.

She speaks. "I am sorry for your loss." It's a voice of angels, sweet, a high ringing note, bringing down a clarity of purpose, the soothing balm of knowledge. Everyone is dead, nothing matters.

Zero.

Everyone is dead, and there is no fighting it. Better to put them out of their misery, end their suffering, free them from a world that is nothing but pain.

The metal shutter clatters up. Costecu is staring at me.

"He will help you end their suffering," the decaying angel says to me. A purpose.

He will guide me, show me how to make the word peaceful, one corpse at a time.

Zero.

"Thank you, my dear," he says to the banshee. He opens the door and comes into the room. "As promised, you will be released. Wherever you would like."

She bows her head. Even in my empty-brain state, I know he won't let her go. Costecu always wins. He's won.

"Are you ready to go to work, Lindberg? There are so many people who need your skills. So many people who are...suffering."

Zero. What is Zero? Zero is the meaning of life. There is no meaning.

There is Zero.

Zero mercy, Zero hope, Zero love. Zero.

"Yes."

"Excellent."

CHAPTER ELEVEN

Aideen

The conference room is too bright and too cold, like they always are. It's something about how conference rooms everywhere are constructed. The shiny wood table, the chairs that are too uncomfortable to sit in for long, even though they look nice, the way the sun always shines through the windows right in your face no matter where you sit. They are universally horrible.

Safiya sits across from me, back to the windows so the sun doesn't shine on her face. She got herself a cup of the bad instant coffee we make here, while I nurse my own from the fancy metal insulated one I bought for way too much money.

"Oh, shoot, I forgot my laptop. Hold on. Beth?" She pushes a button on the strange type of phone that lives in conference rooms, sitting in the middle of the table like a spider.

"Yes, Miss Baha?"

"Can you bring my laptop to the Jupiter conference room?"

Some bright executive had decided if our conference rooms were named after planets, we'd realize we're all part of the cosmic plan, or some shit like that, and then we'd be more productive. Jupiter is the one I hate the most. Mars at least has a nice color scheme, which doesn't have any red at all.

"I hope this won't take too long," I say into the silence, fidgeting with my mug.

"It shouldn't. We need to get everything down. Are you sure you're okay to talk about this?"

"Oh my god, please stop asking." I close my eyes, then rest my forehead down in my hand. This shouldn't bother me as much as it is. "Sorry, yes. I'm fine, but I really don't want to talk, I want to get out there and...do things."

Beth knocks on the door before Safiya can respond, and she's gestured in. "Thanks, Beth. We'll only be in here a couple of hours. If anyone asks for me, they'll have to wait."

I bite my tongue. A couple of hours is way too long. This shouldn't take more than fifteen minutes. I got kidnapped, I got out, I'm back. Easy. This feeling of impatience is irrational, and I'd do the same thing as her in this position, but I still want to flip the table and go running down to the armory to suit up. Drew is out there waiting for me.

Instead, I take the most aggressive drink of coffee I can. Better get this started. The quicker we start, the quicker it's over. "You ready?"

"One more second," Safiya says, tapping at a couple of keys, opening the reports database and creating a new incident. You'd think saving the world would have less red tape, but it's gotten worse than when I was a regular detective.

I tap my fingers on the table, then stop when I notice what I'm doing.

"Okay. I'm ready. Where do you want to start?"

"I was down in the observation room—"

"Lindberg was in the interrogation room? Could you see him?"

"Yes, obviously. Of course I could see him." Already, I'm in trouble. If I admit what I did, going in without a backup, I could get some sort of reprimand. I'm not sure if I care if that happens. In the few seconds of me trying to figure out a way around it, I do, in fact, stop caring. "I needed to get answers from him, and I didn't want to wait to call someone down. Impatient, stupid, all that, I know."

No need to tell all the truth. The truth that deep down in my belly I wanted to get closer, to see if his penetrating gaze was as intense up close as through the thick glass of the observation room. In all this time, I've never bothered to take stock and wonder what was going through my head when I broke all the rules. No one's ever provoked me into something so reckless before.

"Wait, earlier you told me he broke out of the door?"

"I lied. I was...embarrassed."

"So you went in without backup?" She's looking down at the laptop, fingers tapping away at keys, face inscrutable.

"Yes. Like I said, stupid." I wait for something else, recrimination or accusation, but instead she gestures with her hand to keep going. "Okay. So I went in, and he must have been working at the bonds for a while or something, because after a few minutes of talking—"

"What about?"

"I don't really remember. I was trying to get under his skin. Lay the groundwork for future questioning sessions." As long as she doesn't ask what I was thinking, I'll be okay-ish.

"All right. Continue."

"All of a sudden, he ripped the chair out of the floor—"

"We found the metal had been cut partway, so it was probably pretty easy for him to get out."

"Cut? Someone sabotaged it?"

"Seems that way."

"Jackson. Must have been Jackson. He was down there in the observation room by himself for a bit while I let Lindberg cool off after being moved. You think he cut the metal?"

"But why not let Lindberg out all the way?"

I lean back in my chair, crossing my arms. "I don't know."

"We can come back to that. We're simply getting your story down."

Something about her tone of voice provokes me. "You mean the facts, not a story. I'm telling you what happened."

"Yes, that's what I meant. So, Lindberg pulled the chair out of the floor."

She still hasn't looked at me. Her countenance is calm, and everything appears fine, but I can't shake the feeling there's something else going on here. We're all good at reading people or we wouldn't be in the positions we're in. "Right. And then I'm blacked out, like he slammed me against the wall."

"Ouch."

I continue on my account of what happened, Safiya writing everything out in the report. I presume she's putting down what I say verbatim, without adding any comments. I can't help but feel like I'm being interrogated instead of debriefed.

I make it through how he escaped out of the building, and learned of the police reports that were made as a result of his exit in a public manner out of the lobby and down the street. The organization kept my kidnapping out of the official reports, as they didn't want a missing person bulletin to go out. That could get messy, involving humans in searching for someone kidnapped by Costecu. Trying to explain a vampire and dwarf had taken me would be difficult.

I'm okay with it, because that's how we always handle things, as little human involvement as possible, but it's strange to know, officially I was never gone. If I hadn't gotten out myself, it might've been a while before I'd been rescued, if ever. Not that the humans could have helped.

Safiya is sympathetic when I recount my torture. She glances up at several points, eyeing my fingers, my face, probably trying to gauge if I'm suffering from any PTSD or trauma. If I'd been sitting at home thinking about it, I might not be doing so well, but at least being at work I can focus on the job at hand. As soon as I get out of the stupid debrief session.

There are a lot of questions regarding Costecu's base, how many people I saw, how much of the layout I can remember. I end up drawing a map of the parts I'd been in, as much as I remember.

My mind wanders back to Drew. I'm letting the routine of debriefing calm my worries, but he's still out there. Waiting for me, depending on me. If there was any point where I'd abandon protocol, this is it. Which is crazy. I wouldn't abandon the correct course of action for anyone from my previous relationships, no matter what. Protocol is there for a reason.

"So his command center is right off the main hall? That doesn't seem smart," she says as I'm explaining where I met Costecu.

"Yeah. I think it's...he's like back in medieval times. It's an audience chamber, almost. You want that to be front and center, right? So, when we do assault, with any luck he'll be right there, and we can take him out."

She makes a note, and I hope it says "We're going to take him out." I keep recounting how Drew helped me get out although I didn't know it at the time. How I got a ride and made it all the way back here.

"And then people started shooting at me."

"Yeah. About that." She pauses to look sheepish. "At the time we had intelligence, obviously faulty, you'd defected. I was here at the time, and I didn't believe it for one second. I saw the tape of

Lindberg pulling you out through the lobby, and then we had some footage of him outside, driving away with you. There was a red-light camera that picked you up not far from here before we lost you, and you seemed super pissed."

"I was."

"Still, there were...vocal people. It was all an act. Jackson, among them."

"Bet the little fucker was worried he'd get caught. There were other people? Who?" I take another angry drink of coffee. It's starting to get lukewarm. I can't believe there are people here who'd think I'd defect, after everything I've done for this place.

"We can talk about it later."

"Damn straight we will."

"Please, don't get derailed. I'm anxious to see if you survive." It's meant as a joke, and she smiles a fraction, but it doesn't deflect all my anger at finding out that my loyalty is perceived as flexible.

I recount how I escaped, stole a car, at which she raises her eyebrows, and drove to the two highways with no idea of what I'd find there, only suspicions. I leave out the part where I yelled at the cricket, and all the crazy twisty feelings upon seeing Drew again and being carried to his SUV.

Then I have to get even vaguer. The thought of telling anyone that I had sex with Drew makes me want to squirm, and not in the good way he does. I don't know why, but it feels wrong. Dirty. I've slept with people before, of course, who hasn't, nothing to be ashamed of, but this one is unprofessional, to say the least. Having sex with someone who'd tortured you, someone you thought might be an enemy asset, someone who you'd watched kill a dragon with his bare hands? That's not wholesome or romantic.

Remembering how his whole body was straining, taut and hard, pulling off the jaw of the dragon—after having killed three other people—and then how clean he was after the shower, the way the light hit his muscles, gleaming and strong, oh so powerful...

I'm fucking losing my mind. Why I'm so inflamed for Drew is beyond my comprehension. He's nothing but a hulking brute who hits everything and demands my attention every second I'm with him. I like calm men. Men who want to talk about politics over coffee, exactly like the last guy I dated. Robert. He was kind. He bought me flowers for Valentine's Day. He had a dog. We had nice sex.

He would've been murdered at the cabin within the first two minutes. He wouldn't've made it to the cabin at all. He never looked at me with burning desire before tossing me onto a bed as if I were nothing more than a rag doll, and then fu—

"Aideen?"

"Huh?" I drag my mind back to the present, away from Drew and his muscles and his powerful—damn it, focus. "Sorry, I was...thinking."

"You were saying he killed a dragon, a species we haven't seen in the states at all, with his bare hands?"

"Oh, yeah. Yup. I mean, I helped a little, but he ripped the thing's jaw right off, and then shot it through the underside of the mouth."

"You helped?"

"Yeah, uh, I uh..." It's embarrassing to admit when I lose control. It shouldn't control me, I should control it, and I don't like it when I lose control. It shows lack of mental fortitude. "I bit him on the back of his neck."

Safiya glances up again, tilting her head to the side. "You went selkie?"

"Yeah."

"That's not like you at all."

She doesn't have as much hesitation about using her powers as I do. She works out a lot, is at the gym almost every minute she's not at work, using the opportunity to show off her speed and strength. As a djinn, she likes the attention as much as she likes to make people feel good. It makes her fun at parties, but also a bit stressful because of all the attention. I'm not a fan of attention.

"I was...desperate."

"Hm."

After that, it's pretty easy to tell the rest. How after the fight all we did was attempt to relax, nothing else happening at all, and then decided it would be a good idea to leave because if some of Costecu's people found us, more would. Then the car crash, my flight into the woods, hitchhiking back, and then finding Jackson in my condo.

"Then I called you, and that's it. You know the rest."

She heaves a breath, finishes typing a few more things, and then steeples her fingers. "This should be enough to convince them. I hope. Can I ask you a few more things about Lindberg? I haven't had face-to-face contact with him in a while, I'd like to try to judge his mental state."

"You had face-to-face meetings?" Of course, she must have. It would've been stupid not to every once in a while.

"Only a couple times after he made contact and said he wanted to help us. How did he seem to you, personality-wise?"

I rest my elbows on the table and think for a second. "Direct. Confident. Domineering, but with a touch of humor, like maybe he's using it to cover stuff up, feelings he doesn't want to think about."

"Makes sense. Probably a coping mechanism. He was that way from the start."

Something about her tone of voice focuses my attention. "From the start?"

"Yeah, you know. When he was assigned to me. The few times I talked to him. Very offhanded, in an oddly direct way."

"You could say that," I reply, thinking that offhanded would be the opposite word I'd use to describe him, based on all his hands-on groping. I can still feel his handprint on my thigh. Of all the stuff we did, that one is the most real. I catch myself rubbing the area and stop.

"You wouldn't?"

"I guess I'd say he was direct. Maybe it had to do with the situation, but he was always calling me out, or telling me exactly what to do. There wasn't much hesitation at all." I keep thinking about everything else we did where we weren't talking, and how all the same stuff applies. He didn't hesitate at all.

"Hm, that's a bit of a change then."

That weird tone is still there, and I can't put my finger on what's going on. "I don't think it's necessarily a bad thing."

"No, not necessarily. He might be more comfortable in his situation, or perhaps things are more urgent, so he doesn't have time to play around anymore."

The words are innocuous enough, but the way she's holding herself is leading me down a path I don't want to think about. She keeps rubbing her hand across her left wrist, catching herself, and then doing it again. It's the exact same thing I was doing with my thigh. I have to know.

"I wouldn't say he wasn't playful," I say, watching her face. "It wasn't a subtle playfulness, though. He flirted with me a lot, which I thought was odd considering we were supposed to be on opposite sides, but it makes sense."

For the tiniest of seconds, her eyes flick down to her wrist as she touches it again, then everything is back to normal. But it's enough for me to understand, with lightning certainty, what she's thinking about. More specifically, who she's thinking about.

"You didn't mention that," she says, putting her hands back on the keyboard.

"I didn't think it mattered. He was trying to get me worked up. Not really relevant to what happened."

"Did you?"

"Did I what?"

"Get worked up?"

Oh hell. Fucking hell, she slept with him. It all clicks together: the voice, the look, the touching of the wrist, I knew it, but I didn't want to believe it. She's kept it a secret because that would be a terrible breach of protocol, but boy did she ever sleep with him, and she's trying to figure out if I slept with him, too.

Shit, when was the last time they had sex? It doesn't matter. It's not like we're dating. Are they dating? There's no way. It was a one-time thing, adrenaline was high, it was just sex. Hot, powerful, mind-blowing sex, but that's it. He probably has sex with a lot of women. I mean he's seven feet of muscle, confidence, and beard. Who could resist him?

Fuck, fucking...fuck. She can't find out. Shit, I need to answer the question.

"I was pretty stressed out and worried, and he was aggressive, so yes, I did get angry and upset a few times." I'm impressed with how casual and level-headed I sound, what with my heart swimming in my stomach. "It kept me more off-balance than I should've been, which was likely his goal."

"What about in the cabin? Were you worried at all about going to sleep with a potentially dangerous man right there?"

That's not subtle. I have this weird urge to hint, throw little breadcrumbs out, but that would be insane. There's no reason for me to risk my career because of some spur of the moment sex. It was only sex. It would have been a fun week, and then we would have gone our ways, and everything would've been back to normal.

Except for the whole being hunted by an ancient vampire thing, and the part where he said we were running away together. That was only the situation, the adrenaline, the danger. The only reason I know anything about him is from his dossier. I don't know his favorite color or song, how can there be any sort of relationship?

In the cold light of day, I ask myself, do I want a relationship? Doubt chews my guts, mixed with disbelief at how stupid I'd have to be to run away with a guy I've known for a handful of days. A man who pulled out my toenail, for fuck's sake.

A hot, powerful, man who pinned me to the bed and took me like a bull in heat.

"At that point I didn't have much of a choice," I reply to the question Safiya asked. It's a wonder my voice doesn't crack. "It was either try to stay awake in case it was a long con and he was going to hurt me, about which I could've done nothing, or try to sleep and be recharged the next day. I was pretty exhausted."

"And he didn't bother you at all? Break into your room at night, try to molest you when showering, nothing like that?"

Those are really specific questions. I could push, I suppose, or accuse, try to figure out what's going on, try to get her to admit it, but that doesn't seem like a good idea right this second. With the way my own emotions are swimming in my head, and the many complications prodding would conjure, I shouldn't. I can't. Not right now. It was just sex. "Not at all. Why?" Later.

"Making sure you're okay," she replies, typing away. "Making sure he hasn't gone too far. You can tell me, you know? It's nothing to be ashamed of."

Maybe she suspects. I caught her in it, maybe she's caught me. I can't ask. I take my hand off my thigh once again. "Nothing happened. So yeah, nothing to be ashamed of."

"Okay. Good."

"Okay."

"Fine."

I wait to see if she says anything else. "Are we done?"

"Yes, I think so." Her words are clipped as she closes the laptop and stands up. "Do you still intend to mount an assault on the base to rescue Lindberg?"

"To bring down Costecu," I reply, noticing the trap. "Yes, of course."

"Then give me some time to distill this into an easily digestible report. I'm sure you'll want to run it up the chain of command, like protocol demands?"

"Yes."

"Fine."

"Okay."

She marches out of the room, leaving a cloud of obvious resentment behind.

I rub my thigh.

I'm going to need more coffee.

CHAPTER TWELVE

Druain

It's as if I'm back in time. My old house, the house I grew up in, sits in front of me like a long-lost dog. With the lawn out front I cut with our old electric lawn mower, always needing to have the blades sharpened. The chain metal fence with the gate, the latch stiff and so difficult to open. The window to my room on the second floor, the curtains that changed every year because my mother spent every free second she could sewing things.

My father worked a lot. He almost always came home after dinner, or there would be the occasional stretch of a week where he'd be traveling and we wouldn't see him at all. My brother, sister, and I thought he worked for a bank. He didn't.

We each had our own room, eventually. I was the oldest, my sister was four years younger, and my brother was six years younger. They shared a room until he turned five, and then my parents remodeled a small storage area to turn it into a bedroom for him. He never liked it, but he hated sharing a room and sleeping in a bunk bed even more.

I'm standing outside the house in my head, while still sitting in a chair in a dungeon, with my hands nailed to the wood.

As I stare at my window, awash in memories, the curtain twitches, and then my younger self peers out from the other side of the glass. Sixteen, full of anger, desperation, and teen angst. Wanting to be free, whatever that meant at the time. Too stupid to realize freedom means responsibility.

With a sickening flash, I realize what this day is. I could never forget it, as much as I try. It's burned into the surface of my mind like a brand, a reminder, a reason to do what I need to do.

I'd gotten in a fight with my mother over something pointless. She didn't want me wearing the style of jeans fashionable at the time. She told me she had common sense, and I yelled about being oppressed and misunderstood. If only.

My father wasn't supposed to be home that day. He said he would be in Singapore. I never found out if that was true.

The world spins underneath my feet like a carousel, directing my attention down the street. There's the car, the old burgundy red four-door, the one we never rode in because it was always at the airport, or at his office. When my father was home, we still took the minivan. He kept his car spotless and didn't like us messing it up.

He parallel parked on the street, wedging between the cars of our neighbors with practiced ease.

My father was large. He was also a dwarf, as was my mother, and their parents, and their parents. Pure blood is a badge of honor in some circles. I never cared. Blood purity didn't let me wear a nose ring or dye my hair, and after this day my whole will was bent to a different goal than starting a family.

My adolescent face in the window disappears, because he knows he's going to get in trouble. Disrespecting our parents was one of the worst things to do, and the stuff I'd called my mother was anything but respectable. She could still hand out punishment, but I was in the middle of my growth spurt, taller than she was, and I nearly outweighed her. I was all arms and legs, though, and hadn't started to fill out. I wouldn't do that until after.

As my father mounted the steps, I half expect to float along behind him, like an unseen camera, but as the door closed, I need to signal my feet to suggest they walk forward. The door melts away as soon as I touch it, and I drift inside.

The inside of the house is the same as always, although a bit unhinged from time. That end table wasn't there when I was sixteen, and the entrance floor flickers between the hardwood and the tile, two different coverings from two different periods. The air has a slight tinge of blue, as if smoke or fog is obscuring the edges.

The rumble of conversation comes from the kitchen where my mother is making dinner. I wander into the doorway but can't see what she's making. Her hands fade to nothing as they hover over the counter, and even as close as I am, I can't understand what they're saying to each other.

Of course. It's a memory. I wasn't down here. My brain is filling in the gaps, substituting placeholders for reality. Outside the window over the sink is the banshee. She watches me, tears running down her face.

She shouldn't be here, wasn't here, but I feel no shock or anger. I'm an observer, nothing more. Neither my brain nor any of my organs are here to flood me with adrenaline.

My parents' hazy conversation continues, my father standing stock still, my mother not moving save her arms waving over the counter. It's surreal and disturbing, bringing my parents back to the forefront of my mind in an unpleasant way.

Drawn by a string I can't see, my fake body is pulled out of the kitchen, up the stairs, the creaky step not making any noise as I pass it, and into my room. My teenage self is on the bed, pretending to read a battered copy of *I, Robot*, waiting for the hammer of inevitable punishment. Up here, the murmur of their voices is the same volume as it was downstairs.

Devoid of the emotions and hormones plaguing every young person, I was able to pay attention to the sounds I unconsciously dismissed last time. Or perhaps they're more made-up hallucinations based off of what's about to happen.

A fleet of vehicles came down the road, which was quiet most of the time. It was a safe neighborhood, a few streets away from main roads, with not a lot of traffic besides people going to and from work.

Five SUVs coming down the block made a lot of noise. They didn't bother to park, pulling up in the middle of the road. They knew it wasn't going to take a lot of time. My gaze is drawn to the window. The curtains dissipate like fog. The banshee is standing on the road, in the midst of the convoy, staring at me again. She's doing this, subjecting me to this horror I've tried to banish from my mind.

People get out of the SUVs. They aren't human, as much as they might try to appear that way. Subtle things are off. Eyes, noses, fingers, the way they walk.

The front door downstairs shatters inward, blown off the hinges. My father shouts in alarm, my little brother screams, and chaos breaks like a tsunami over a floodwall.

My dream-self leaps from the bed and in two steps is at the door to my room. Go help, I shout, but no words come out. Help, you can make a difference, you can save everyone, but it's too late. I can't help or save anyone, because this has already happened.

It happened, and I tucked it away in my mind and I never pull it out, but then the banshee cracked me open like a walnut and pulled me back in.

The edges of my vision turn black, sharp flickers of red in the corners, and time pauses. The banshee is next to me. I reach out to strangle her, but my hands do nothing. They either pass through her, or won't grip her neck, or never move, or all of the above.

Time snaps back, rewinding a few seconds before diving forward like a broken rubber band. My past turns and wrenches at the window as the figurative and literal flames leap to the front of my eyes. They've set the house on fire. Shouting and gunshots ring from below. I watch myself leap from the second story, roll on the ground, and sprint off.

"They're all dead," the banshee says as the flames lick at me, their heat something I feel but am not affected by. "You ran away."

I can't speak. My lips won't move as the flames eat me, the shrieking dies away, and the fuzzy edges fade into grey, then white, and then black.

After a few seconds, or a few years, the black brightens, and the familiar and recent surroundings of my cabin swim into focus. Warm colors, a fireplace I never used as much as I wanted, a place of peace when everything got too much.

"You killed her," the banshee says, standing on the other side of the front window. I can hear her clear as a bell, not with my ears, but with my mind.

There I am, sitting on the chair and reading my book. Zero must be sleeping in the other room. If my memory is correct, this is the night where I got groceries, except the bodies of the four who came before Gil are already piled on the floor in front of the fireplace.

The light in the cabin goes dim as the sun sets faster than it should. A fire springs up in the fireplace, but what rolls off of it is cold, not heat. If I could shiver, I would. It's bone-piercing. The banshee is beside me.

"You killed them, and in doing so, killed her."

The cold statement of fact, false on so many levels, does something to me. I rage, rage as much as someone who is trapped in their mind and cut off from emotions can rage. An ember of warmth tickles my chest.

I'm pulled down the hallways and through the door into the room where Zero is sleeping.

"She's been murdered," the banshee says without words.

Blood streaks the sheets, splattered across the walls. It drips from the window behind the bed, drops puddle on the floor. Zero is dead, naked, sliced by a thousand cuts, deep and shallow, across her skin. Her eyes are open, and she stares at me, grotesque and obscene.

"You killed me," her lips say, her eyes glassy and ice blue. Unnatural.

I fight down a surge of rage. This isn't real. I protected Zero from everything thrown at her. I saved her, and she's still alive. I would do it all again, because she deserves to live, even if I die. There's no place in this word for someone who only knows how to hurt people, but there's plenty of space for someone who helps others. I'll hurt whoever I have to if it means Zero will be safe.

The ember of determination sparks, a strike of steel against flint, the sharp sound of a fire igniting. The flames of my anger burst up into my skull, and the blue-tinged fog shrinks away from me.

"No," I say. Like a volcano cracking the earth, red-hot determination floods through my bones.

The banshee blinks, staggers back a step.

Zero sits up and screams. "You killed me."

"No." My hands are corporeal as they close around the throat of the banshee and squeeze.

Her skin is wet, rubbery, but thin as paper, her bones underneath brittle. I can snap her neck in an instant, but she disappears before I can follow through. I swing around to Zero, still sitting up and screaming like the dead. The banshee is outside the bloody window, screaming as well.

I'm hallucinating, trapped in my mind knowing none of this matters. What matters is Zero right here and needing help. As long as I can help, in whatever form I'm able, I will.

I snatch her up, fling her over my shoulder, and tap her butt. "Hush, Zero. You're fine. It's all in my mind."

As soon as the words leave my lips, all the slices and blood vanish from her skin, and she stops her wailing.

"It's as easy as that?" I say to the banshee, still outside and still screaming, a note of anger and despair resonates in my teeth, but it can't break through the wall of rage beating inside me. All the blood disappears from the floor and walls of the room, leaving it as fresh as the day I moved in.

I carry Zero out of the bedroom, intending to take her out of the cabin and go anywhere I can to get away from the banshee. If this is my mind, then I'm going to make it a fortress.

Two steps down the hall, and the flames from the fireplace leap across the hearth and set the bodies aflame with a cold, blue heat. The disfigured bodies roll across the entrance of the hallway before I can get there, the flame lapping at the ceiling.

It's all in my mind, none of it is real. I step forward, through the flame, except I don't. I can't. The heat and the cold and the roaring sound push me back, again and again, as Zero lies draped over my shoulder, placid as a baby.

"Get out of my way," I shout, kicking at the corpses, trying to push them away. The flame grabs my leg and won't let go, licking at the tan of my slacks. I shake the leg, put out the flame, kick again, catch fire again. "This is my mind. Get out."

The banshee wavers on the other side of the wall of fire, crying and wailing in that note that attempts to worm back into my brain.

"Dead," she keens. "They're all dead."

"No." I refuse to give in.

"Your parents."

"Shut up."

"Your siblings."

"Costecu killed them, not me." The flames seem to be ebbing, although I still can't pass through. I focus, hard, refusing to give in, needing to get out.

Zero starts kicking and squirming. "Let me go. Who are you? Let me go."

"Not happening, Zero."

"Please don't kill me."

"I'm not going to kill you," I grumble, gnashing my teeth. "Stay calm."

She stops her struggles, but the flames shoot back up, stronger than before. The banshee sighs, an eerie sound that scrapes across my bones.

I focus on putting the flames out, and Zero starts to fight again. I focus on calming her, and the fire licks at my feet. So that's how it's going to be.

I'm not strong enough to fight the banshee yet. She's caught me, but I'm still here, and the shocked expression on her face tells me she must be fighting, too. It's my mind, my stubborn and stone-strong mind. I only need more time. Like healing bones, if I keep using it, I can win.

I make sure it's clear I'm not running away, then turn and march into the bathroom. Shutting the door, I set Zero on her feet, facing me. She stares at me, eyes clear, face empty of an emotion or thought. While she's as gorgeous in my mind as she is in real life, and being naked doesn't help, this isn't really Zero. It's a vessel waiting for my mind to fill it.

I could give her clothes, but this is my brain and my fantasy, so she'll stay naked. No one has to know. Except I'm definitely telling her when I get out of this, if only to watch the war of emotions march across her face.

The noise of the banshee and the flames are crackling in the hallway. The fists of the dead corpses are pounding at the door. I turn on the shower. Water will keep us from burning alive. It makes sense.

"You'll never get in here," I call to the air. "You better leave before I get my strength back, because then I'm coming for you."

The water runs hot, the opposite temperature of the flames, and I strip off my clothes and tug Zero under the shower with me. Her eyes don't leave me for one second, as if I might look away and she'll disappear, which could be what happens here.

"Don't worry, Zero," I say, thumbing her cheek as the water darkens her hair further, plastering it to her skin. "I won't let you get hurt."

"Don't let me get hurt," she echoes.

"I won't." I hug her. I realize I haven't hugged her in the real world. It's an intimacy we haven't shared, and something I crave. I hold onto that feeling as I hold onto her. She's warm, but not as warm as life, and soft, but not as soft as tenderness. It's a whispering promise of the future, as long as I can get out of here.

The sounds of flame and screaming start to fade, slow as ice across a windowpane, but I can wait.

I will get out of here, and then Costecu is going to pay.

CHAPTER THIRTEEN

Aideen

"Frank," I shout, storming into my office suite and slamming the door behind me. "We've got work to do. Are you up for it?"

"Of course, Miss Duffy," he replies, sitting up straight behind his desk, a consummate professional assistant. He grabs a pen, ready to write. "What do you need?"

A heavy drink. "I need to get transcripts of every conversation Druain Lindberg has had with Safiya Baha, and I don't care they're confidential. I need all the numbers for every member of the board, so I can call them personally. Who's in charge of Jackson's squad now? I need the squad leader on duty up in my office in five minutes. I need a coffee that isn't damned trash, I don't care where you get it from. I need..." It's a risk, but I think it's worth it. He looks up, pen poised, waiting for the next order. I pull my condo key out of my pocket. "I need you, don't send anyone, it needs to be you, to go to my condo, get in my closet, find a little wood box about this big, and bring it to me. Don't tell anyone, don't open it, don't let anyone take it. I need it as soon as you get the rest done."

"Yes, ma'am," he says, jotting down more notes, unperturbed. If I end up in an even more clandestine job, I've got to get him to come with me. If I asked him to eat his cat because it was mission critical, he would.

"Good." I step into my private office, shut the door, then open it again to stick my head out. "Thanks."

"No problem. I assume you don't want any visitors or phone calls?"

"Correct. Get me those transcripts before you go."

"You got it," he beams, brimming with unrestrained and helpful energy.

I shut the door again and plop into my chair. I need something to do. I've been tossed into a river and need a log to cling onto. The moment I get those transcripts I'll be reading them for any hint or clue, more out of a sense of curiosity than anything else. I have to know. Not that it matters if he's slept with her, of course, we're all adults. But I need to know.

The five minutes before the on-duty squad leader arrives feels like a vast amount of time, stretching in front of me for all eternity. I stare vacantly out my window at the cityscape at night. Last time I looked out this window, my world was one hundred percent different. I was about to capture Costecu and Lindberg together. Instead of being in the throes of celebration, lounging in my tub with a whole bottle of wine for an entire day, I've been through the ringer.

A city at night isn't that dark. There are streetlights everywhere, glowing orange in the night, and the streets are easy to trace. Plenty of people are working as well. The stars aren't visible through the haze of civilization.

Drew is out there. Right over there. My eyes follow the highway up to the rough area in the industrial area where Costecu is buried. A nest of villainy. I'm being melodramatic.

My phone beeps. I spin and push the button. "Yes?"

"Mr. Esmail is here to see you, at your request," Frank's voice chirps out.

"Okay, send him in."

The lithe form of the sphinx, one of the six squad leaders, steps through the door and then drapes himself into the chair opposite my desk. "You called?"

Omari's insouciance is sometimes endearing, but normally infuriating. In this moment, it's the latter.

"If you need to go out, how quick can you assemble your group?"

"What kind of engagement?" he asks, studying his fingernails.

"Heavy duty raid. I can't tell you, because it's not approved, but it would be raiding Costecu's home base."

"Hmm," he sticks his pinky in the corner of his mouth, eyes rolled to the ceiling, thinking. "I mean, we'd need more people."

"Obviously." I cross my arms and try not to sigh. Pushing this guy would be counterproductive. If you've ever tried to get a cat to do something, it's the same thing. If he wasn't so clever, he'd be more annoying than his worth.

"Not saying my people aren't good. They're good, the best. But Costecu's got a lot of people." He changes to chewing on the next nail.

"Yes."

"Maybe a couple hours? Three? Depending on how long it takes for everyone else to get here. The other teams."

"Three hours?" That's a long time, but by the time I get the higher-ups convinced and signed on, it might not be that long after all. Except I have to wait until they say okay before I can get him rolling.

"Maybe a couple." He shrugs with one shoulder. I want to punch his angular face.

"Okay."

"Why? Are we going? I heard you know where he's at." His nose twitches.

"No, and no comment. Not yet anyway. Let's say, if you got your people ready ahead of time, I'd owe you a favor. Unofficially."

"A favor? What kind of favor?" He looks at me out of the corner of his eye, pretending to study the arm of the chair.

I roll my eyes. "I'll take you out for sushi."

"Sakura?"

"Sakura? That's like two hundred...fine."

"Awesome." He slides out of the chair and pads out of the door without saying goodbye. Damn cat.

My phone beeps again. "Yes, Frank?"

"I have those files for you, if you're ready."

"Yes, please, and don't tell me how you got them." He opens the door and sets the folder down on my desk. They're hardcopy? No digital?" I can't resist, opening the manilla folder and starting to read.

"Afraid so, Ma'am."

"Ugh. Thanks again. Let me know when you're back right away, okay?"

"Of course." He's out the door, leaving me in peace, without lingering.

The interviews are dry and boring. Nothing in there at all to indicate any sort of relation, sexual or otherwise. Maybe I was wrong, except her body language was all over it, the same thing I kept doing. I know that look, because I'm feeling it.

It was just sex. Nothing special. I want more, and I'll bet she does, too.

Did they start right from the beginning? Did she go through this by-the-book interview, and then meet him later that night? There's no possibility the transcripts were falsified, because someone else would watch the video later and type it all up. Unless she bribed whoever typed it.

Okay, I'm being paranoid. This is stupid. So they had sex, so what? It doesn't matter. Anyone can have sex with anyone, as long as they consent. People are having sex right now. I wish I was having sex. With Drew. For a long, long time.

I get out of my chair and pace the room to try to work off the energy concentrated between my thighs. I'm going to rescue him, and then he'll be super grateful, and then he'll reward me with his body, like in those trashy romance books. Except I guess I'm the guy and he's the girl. That's weird.

Grabbing a throw pillow off the couch no one uses, I shove it over my face. A scream or two later and I feel a bit better. Back to the chair and the transcripts.

There's nothing in them at all. They might as well be two people who have never met before and are having casual conversations. Conversations about Costecu's operation. Almost all the leaks I got are in here, every one. Some much earlier than they arrived at my desk, along with some stuff that I could've used. I'm not sure if I'm angrier at someone deciding what information I needed when, or I can't tell when they started fucking.

I gather up everything and shove it in my drawer, then take it back out and get up to shove it in my filing cabinet, way in the back, along with the Christmas cards work colleagues sent me I've never opened.

Opening the door to see why Frank isn't back yet, frustrated and pent-up, I almost bump into him. He joggles my wooden box in his hand, startled, and I grab at it.

"Oh shoot," he exclaims as I snatch it and hold it close. "I'm so sorry, Miss Duffy. You surprised me."

"It's okay, Frank. It's fine. Thanks. Is that my coffee?"

"Yes, ma'am." He holds out the cup in his other hand. It's warm, large, and perfect.

"You're the best."

"I'll get those phone numbers for you."

"Okay." I retreat into my office and set both precious items down on my polished wood desk. Pushing my laptop out of the way, I take a quick sip of the coffee, and then pause to study the box. I don't pull it out often because what it represents is more than a bit scary. It's myths and realities boiled down to one item. If anyone with bad intentions got it, I'd be in serious trouble.

I unlatch the little brass swinging lock, swing it up, and lift the lid. The silver pendant is the same as I remember it, as it always is. A black stone, set in a nest of silver wires twisted into an artistic rendering of waves. The wires aren't important, but the stone is.

My essence is in it, my selkie heritage and powers. Without it, I'm still special, set apart from humans. With it resting around my neck, strung on the short silver chain, I can draw on hidden reserves. I don't like using them. It feels...primitive.

I stare at it a while longer, gathering the courage to pick it up. Tying my hair back into a ponytail gives me more time to stall. I'm not afraid of it, but I'm afraid of what it represents.

It's heavier than it should be for its size as I lift it from the padding. The sparse light of my office is drawn to the stone. It wants to be worn. I run my thumb across the cool surface, then pocket the talisman, close the box, and put it in my bottom drawer, which I lock.

Frank's email with all the numbers pings in the bottom right corner of my screen, and I'm glad for the distraction. Anything to not think about what that pendant means.

I pull the numbers and scan the names attached, trying to decide who's going to be the best one to start with. I make a list cross-referencing those who're most receptive to taking proactive actions and those who have no qualms about those actions being aggressive. A lot of the names are the same.

No one really knows who's on the "board of directors." For safety reasons they all use aliases when communicating with us, along with a host of other precautionary measures, but a lot of them have European accents. Being in the American side of the system sometimes has disadvantages. We need more advocates.

Two hours later I'm no closer to my goals. A couple have indicated cautious acceptance, but only if the others will get on board. I can't get anyone to outright side with me on my quest to free Drew. I've told them all it's an assault on Costecu, which they all agree with, but want more time. They want to gather more intelligence, figure out numbers, layouts, resources, all the prudent things I would also agree with if we had all the time in the world.

Drew doesn't. He needs me now, but I can't tell anyone that.

I slam the Bluetooth headset down in frustration after the last one, shattering the cheap plastic. The chair creaks as I lean back as far as I can, putting my feet up on my desk and staring at the ceiling. There's got to be some way I can get Drew out.

Of course, I could go and get him myself. There's nothing stopping me from driving over there and fighting everyone inside. They'll take turns, I'm sure, let me rest for a bit between fights, it will all be honorable. Right. Costecu will give him up when he sees how determined I am. I might be so scary I won't have to fight anyone.

There's an idea. I shouldn't fight anyone. I should sneak in, find out where Drew is, and sneak back out. They're in such disarray, with their second in command a sudden enemy, they'll never notice someone else walking around.

My phone beeps again, interrupting my oh so clever planning. I wrench myself upright to hit the button. "Yes?"

"Miss Baha is here."

"What for? Oh. The report, probably. Uh, that's fine."

The door opens and she walks in, more formal than Omari. She's a professional.

"I filed it," she says, sitting down, back straight.

"Okay. I already called everyone," I admit. "The ones in the States weren't all happy about being woken up."

"You should have waited," she says, brows furrowing. "I could've helped. What did they say?"

"Basically, it's a no-go. They want to take time, plan, and get everything right. Some were open, but only if everyone else was on board."

"But Costecu could up and leave. He should if he's smart."

"I know. I told them."

She growls in frustration. "He's going to get away. It'll take forever to find him again, especially if we lose Lindberg. Because he's our source," she adds.

"They seem to feel he's not as important as all that. Apparently, they have faith in my abilities to pick up the pieces and start over again, if needs be."

I'm looking at her, and she's looking at me. Neither of us flinch. We're simply two concerned people worried about an asset who could get killed. Nothing else.

"I was thinking about a covert action," I say after what feels like an eternity, tenting my fingers and swiveling in my chair. We could sit here and play chicken with each other all day, but every second is another second Drew is in trouble.

"Oh?" Her eyebrows raise a tiny amount, so infinitesimal I could be imagining it.

"I think he's important enough to risk it, whether they do or not. They're not down here in the trenches with us."

She purses her lips. It doesn't take much thought to imagine what's going on in her head. It's the same thing going on in my head.

"Can we do it with two people?" she asks.

"Two?"

"I'm going."

"Omari would probably help."

"Too risky. He's good and all, but the more people the more danger. Do you want to put other people's lives and careers at risk?"

"Is two enough?" I guess we're planning an incursion.

"It's the perfect number. The two of us can provide good cover, but not we're not too many to be noticeable."

"When's the last time you were in the field?"

She rolls her eyes. "Please. I'm in better shape than you. I should ask the same thing."

"I'm fine. Maybe I'm not a gym junkie, but I can keep up. Maybe you forgot everything I went though, and I'm totally fine."

"Are you?"

"Yes." Now it's my turn to roll my eyes. "You're not going without me. This is my operation."

"He's my contact."

"You said it yourself, two are better than one. We're both going."

"Okay."

Now that I've said it, it feels real. It was a thought before, something to ponder, but if I'm being truthful, it was always happening. Having some backup can't hurt.

"Do you need to do anything?" I ask her, implying a whole host of things. Drew might be dead, we might not come back, if he's alive and we do come back, we might be worse than fired, we might not make it out of the building if someone catches us. We're walking into a deathtrap.

"I'm going to go home and change into something more practical. You should too?"

She has a good point. I don't need to be wearing work slacks and a fancy blouse to sneak into the enemy base. She might be tricking me so she can go by herself, but I'll follow anyway. It's a minor risk. "Fine. Meet you back here in thirty? In the garage."

"Okay."

I watch her leave, consumed with thoughts about getting to Drew first. It's a thing. I have to be the one, which is utterly ridiculous and petty, because the only thing that should matter is he gets rescued. Along with anyone else down there who needs it, sure, and we stop Costecu, yes. Those are good reasons. Saving people is worth more than a job.

Saving Drew is worth five jobs. I lose myself in imagining how appreciative he'll be again, then shake my head and blink to clear the horny-webs. Got to get ready.

Pushing out of my chair, I grab my keys from the drawer and pop out into the front of the office. "Frank?"

"Yes, ma'am?"

"I'm going to go do something. If anyone asks, I'm here but doing something super serious. I cannot, under any circumstances, be disturbed. No one can know I'm not here."

"You got it. I'll Gandalf anyone who tries to get in."

"What?"

"'You shall not pass'?" he quotes in a low voice, raising an imaginary staff over his head.

"You're strange, Frank. If I'm not back in a day or so...well then it won't matter. I'm sure you'll be able to find a new job here. You've been exceptionally helpful."

"Should I be worried?" he asks, eyes crinkling in concern. If he's asking a question, he must be *really* worried.

"Nope. See you later."

I avoid running down the hallway to the elevator, but as soon as it deposits me in the garage I sprint to my car and drive home as quickly as possible.

I'm not going to let Safiya beat me.

I'm not going to let Drew down.

CHAPTER FOURTEEN

Druain

I'm not sure how much time has passed. Me and imaginary Zero, standing in the shower, the hot water keeping the flames of ice away. She stares at me the whole time, like some lost puppy waiting for a treat because she sat on command.

"Not much longer, Zero," I say, running a knuckle down her cheek, tracing the path of the water. As much as I want to stay here, it's a trap as much as the banshee's flames and memory replays are. I need to get out and get back to myself. Wherever that is.

I concentrate, not sure on what, but I pretend my brain is getting more like a rock. A stone. No, a boulder. Huge and impenetrable. Nothing can turn me to dust, nothing will get in my way, and nothing will stop me from my goal. I'm going to roll down this mountain, crush everything and everyone in my way, and then I'll have some steak for dinner. Medium rare.

The edges of my vision crackles like paper, or maybe glass, curling in while smoke fills the bathroom. Except it's not smoke. It's things fading away.

Zero glimmers like a glass doll, and I can see the other side of the shower through her. Then I can see through the shower wall.

Costecu is right in front of my face, asking me a question. I have no idea what it is, but my body must, because it answers. I can feel the wind leaving my lungs, my lips moving, throat constricting to form a word. It's all pretty gross when you're inside looking out. One shouldn't be forced to think about how all their muscles move. The subtle sound of a tongue moving is horrifying.

"I need to get back out there, Zero," I say, turning her to face the wall, as if perhaps she can watch, or maybe her watching will give me more power. I miss the real Zero. She has so much anger and determination inside her, but this imaginary one is placid and boring.

"I can hear your thoughts, asshole," she says.

"Zero, you're back."

"I'm you, so I guess you're back. Not all the way though, hmm?"

I watch Costecu pull the nails out of my hands in the real world. It should hurt more than it does. As it is, all I feel is a slight ghosting pressure in my palms. He doesn't give me anything to staunch the bleeding. Severe lack of hospitality there.

His expression is much easier to read when half my brain isn't busy with keeping my heart beating and my lungs breathing, and whatever else bodies do.

"Huh?"

"I said, 'not all the way.' Because you're standing here in the imaginary shower in your imaginary cabin, with your imaginary erection against my imaginary ass, instead of out there killing people."

"I'm only human. Plus, I've still got a banshee in here. Anyway, don't pretend you don't like it."

The banshee in the real world seems worried, but I don't think Costecu notices. He's so caught up in his victory he's got no idea what's going on. Her eyes are fixed on me, and if I didn't know better, I might think she's looking at *me*, not the unresponsive slab of meat my flesh has become.

Zero continues talking. "Technically, I'm you, so you're rubbing up against your own ass."

"My ass feels amazing, then."

Imaginary Zero hmpfs. "Maybe work on getting out so you can touch the real thing."

She's right, of course. I peel my eyes from the scene taking place in the torture room to glance over my shoulder. The flames have made it into the bathroom, but they don't get any closer than about a foot from the shower. The corpses are likewise flailing away, but not making any progress.

"Okay, Zero, we're going to try something."

"About damn time."

"Hush, woman. If you weren't so hot and smart, you'd be seriously annoying." I fling her over my shoulder. She struggles, but not in a serious way. The fun type of way I want her to do every time we interact. It's not fun if it's easy. "When I get out of here, you're getting such a spanking."

"Promises, promises."

Tucking my chin, I focus on the fire in front of me. It's all in my mind, *my* mind, and I can do whatever I want here. I step forward, and the flames ease back, although not without some resistance. It's kind of like pushing against a wall of gelatin: soft and smooshy, but I get the feeling if I went too fast it would suck me in and suffocate me.

One step at a time I push the flames and corpses back. A wailing rises behind me, mixed with the crackling of the fire and the furious grunting of the deceased. If I hadn't experienced all these noises, and more, a hundred times before, it might be disturbing.

I'm in a bubble of clear air, while all around me the forces and manipulations of the banshee try to get to me and Zero. I'm not sure where I'm going, but it would be an accomplishment, symbolically, if I made it out the door of the cabin. Since this whole thing is symbolism anyway, I might as well go for it.

The cabin is burning around me, and more people who are dead and on fire join in beating at the invisible field. I recognize some of them but refuse to let them get to me. None of this is real. As I walk over the charred wooden floor, it turns into beautiful hardwood before flaming back into a burnt mess after I pass. The front door is right ahead.

"Are those your parents?" Imaginary Zero asks, pointing off to the side.

"Not helping. I thought you were on my side."

"She is fighting you for control of me."

I can feel the truth of the words. There's a pressure nesting in my brain, that if I let my concentration slip for a second or two, Zero might stab me in the back. "No one gets to control you but me, Zero."

"Comforting."

The door melts away as I reach to touch it, and as I step out onto the porch, with the sun shining above and the birds singing songs that should be in Disney movies, a small weight lifts from my shoulders.

I glance over my shoulder to see the cabin in the center of a roaring inferno, but the flames don't go outside the walls. The roof collapses as I walk down onto the grass, and the porch catches fire, but no one follows me out.

"I think we might be free," I say to Zero.

"No. You're still here, and not out there."

I turn around to where she's looking, toward the woods. The banshee is out there, weaving among the tree trunks, stalking me but not getting any closer. The trees are opaque, and through them I can see the real world again.

In that real world I'm walking along a stone corridor, which is the same as every corridor in the base. I can't place where it is, but maybe it's the disconnect between me and my body that's making it difficult. I try to do something to maybe stop my legs from moving, like thinking about it really hard, but the only response I can elicit is the most minuscule of a stumble. It's something. I'll come back to it.

It would be more fruitful to get this damn banshee out of my brain. As long as she's in here, things aren't going to get better out there.

"I don't suppose you remember how to kill a banshee?" I ask.

"No. You don't?"

"Can't quite seem to grasp it yet. Probably being blocked. If I put you down, are you going to run away?"

"I guess we'll find out."

I don't like having her slight weight and warmth off my shoulder, but I need to see if I can control her. If I can, then it's two against one, and I like those odds much better. Only fools fight fair. I set her down in front of me, bare feet hitting the grass. Now would be a good time to imagine us up some clothes. In fact, combat gear would be better.

"Sorry to have to do this," I say, and then a moment later she's garbed in full tactical apparel. Somehow, it makes her hotter. The armor is molded to her curves in ways real body armor isn't. As all sorts of fun games we could play run through my mind, I'm interrupted by the banshee flitting behind us, glaring and moaning. I give myself a similar outfit, armor, combat boots, gloves, and several loaded weapons.

"Looks like I'm yours," Zero says, standing firm, no sign of running off.

"Yes, you are." Someday I'm going to say those words to her in the real world.

Through the visual portals of the trees, my outside body enters a cell. Must be in the dungeons somewhere. A creature is strapped to a chair, glaring at me in fear and loathing. The low drone of Costecu's voice is buzzing in my ear, saying something I can't decipher. No time to worry about that. Don't get distracted.

"It might not matter what kills banshees, because this is my brain, and if I believe something will kill them, then in here it'll kill them. Make sense?"

"Works for me," Zero says, checking the rounds in her semi-automatic like a pro.

"Fuck, you're so hot right now."

"Keep it together. Let's go. Whoever kills her gets cunnilingus." She runs off into the woods.

"What? Hey, what if I win? I don't have a vagina." I run off after her, before realizing following behind would be stupid. It's unfortunate I won't get to stare at her butt, but we need to work separately to corner the banshee.

Hey, do we have telepathy in here?

Looks like.

Man, I need to get psychically attacked more often. My brain is awesome.

If I concentrate, I find I can see out of Zero's eyes, but it's disorienting. Having all the trees show me what's going on in the real world is one thing when trying to dodge between them and spot the banshee, but then having Zero's vision on top of that makes me dizzy.

It's easier to assume she knows what she's doing, which she does, because she's me, than to try to direct her. The banshee knows something is up and has stopped showing herself in a weak attempt to frighten me.

Then there's a quiet rumbling, and out from behind every tree pops a decaying corpse, eyes bulging, mouth open, hands reaching.

Zombies?

Seems so. Shoot the head.

I know how to kill zombies, Zero. She's trying to slow me down. Try to get past them, don't waste your time.

"This isn't scary at all," I shout to the woods in general, using my pistol to pop zombie heads. No need to waste the ammo of my bigger guns, though I'm sure I could imagine more. "Have you shot your load already with that whole scene showing me my family dying? You got anything else?"

I've always found it helpful to taunt and belittle your opponent as much as possible. Even if they don't allow themselves to be upset by your words, it's a good way to pump yourself up. Confidence is half of the reason people win fights.

The trees show me reaching for the creature strapped to the chair. It doesn't take a genius to figure out what's going on out there. There's nothing I can do about it, and if I let myself get lost in the tragedy, I won't get out of here. Sometimes people need to be sacrificed. I'll try to figure out who it is later, and maybe give their family some money or something.

The zombies get close, but never manage to touch me. It's a simple matter to shoot myself out of their cordon and leave them behind. As soon as they're out of my line of sight, their moans and groans fade. If I can't see them, they have no power.

I break through the last line of trees, bursting onto the two-lane highway running by my cabin. Zero emerges to my left, a few hundred feet away.

"Which way did she go?" I shout.

Zero shrugs.

This is my brain, my memories she's trying to use against me. "That way." I point up the road to Zero. Toward the spot where Costecu caught up with us after we fled. Most likely the banshee wants to make me feel guilty about how I should've known they were coming and done something more to help Zero. I'm good with what happened, though. After all, she's out there, away from all of this. I did the right thing.

I jog to catch up with the Zero traveling in my mind. She's not perfect, a bit too much like me, but I still want to be close to her. It'll work until I can get the real thing. Not much longer.

The road is showing what's happening on the outside. It's not pleasant. The person strapped to the chair is crying, and my hands are around their throat. I'm choking them to death. Their neck between my fingers ghosts across my senses, but I push it away. Not now. Later I can avenge them. Sorry, random person.

"You're letting them die," Zero pipes up next to me as we jog down the highway.

"Yup. I can't focus on two places at once. If I try to stop that, I won't be able to stop the banshee. It will be a temporary victory."

"That's cold."

"I didn't get where I am by being an empathetic person."

"That's sad."

I wave a dismissive hand at the attempt to detail me. "Not going to talk about this. I do what has to be done. Get out of Zero's head, banshee."

Imaginary Zero wavers, and then smiles. "You're strong of mind, determined, and you work toward the greater good."

"Thanks for the pep talk."

The rest of the trip we travel in silence. There's no sign of the banshee. It's unnerving, but maybe it means she's busy running. She's scared and weak, and I'm going to beat her. The scene in the road is hard to ignore, so I switch to staring at the sky, but then it shows up there, too.

The face of the victim is purple, tongue swollen and hanging out, drool rolling down the corner of their mouth. If I could help it, I tried to snap people's necks instead of choking, which takes too long. Costecu is chuckling and murmuring in my ear like a deranged lover.

"That's gross," Zero says.

"Yeah. Why aren't we at the accident yet? Why don't I teleport us there?"

I pull to a stop and concentrate as Zero stands a few paces in front of me. Nothing happens. I try harder, thinking super hard about transferring us to the crash site.

"You look like you need to shit."

"Thanks, Zero. You're oh so helpful. It's not working. Let's keep running."

We take off at a quicker run, trotting along with renewed determination. After a minute, I break into a sprint. I don't waste breath talking.

Can't get tired here. Run as fast as you can.

We run, feet pelting the pavement, a full out sprint, for longer than I've ever been able to run before. For a moment, I lose myself in the joy of it, the wind against my face, the feeling of freedom, racing Zero in a competition neither of us will win or lose.

The feeling of euphoria evaporates when we round a bend and I recognize the dirt road to my cabin.

"Shit. Did we run in a circle somehow? You can't fight me, so you're going to try to twist me up into knots?" I shout into the air, where the dead and purple face of the captive fills the sky. The grotesque tongue, swollen, dark. The eyes, shot through with burst blood vessels. A slow drip of crimson blood seeping from a nostril. Another horror in my memories I can't ever get rid of.

The vision turns and Costecu's smug countenance comes into view. He says something, but I'm not paying attention.

It doesn't matter.

Soon I'll be free and then I'm going to crush his stupid skull like a cantaloupe in a vise.

CHAPTER FIFTEEN

Aideen

In my condo I change as quickly as possible, picking out black yoga pants and a black top with long sleeves, because if I'm going to be covert, I might as well lean into it. In the bathroom, I stare at my face, and my hair in particular. Inspiration overtakes me, and I fish around in the drawers until I find the scissors. I pull my hair back in one hand like I would to make a ponytail and, with a lot more sawing than I expected, chop off my hair.

The long length feels heavy in my hand when it's free of my head, and for a moment I panic. I haven't had short hair in, well...since I was a kid. One summer my mom got tired of dealing with the tangles and cut it all off. At the time it was almost traumatic, but as summer went on it felt good to have the wind blowing across my neck.

My head might float away, but whether that's from the missing pounds or the crazy sense of euphoria, I'm not sure. I cut off all my hair for no reason because a crazy whim told me to. The edges are ragged as it rests right above my shoulders, and it's nowhere close to professional, but as I bob my head side to side, watching it twirl, it's freeing.

I feel like I can take on the world, so Costecu will be no problem.

Tossing my excised tresses into the trash, I brush away some loose strands on the countertop, but then can't delay any longer. My talisman is tucked under my top, the stone cool against my skin, and I don't remember putting it on, but there it is. I don't want to take it off.

There's nothing I need to take with me but what I have. I'll borrow all the gear from the barracks at work. As long as I have myself and my talisman, I should be fine.

As fine as someone can be sneaking into a place bound to be crawling with enemies who can see, hear, and smell better than I can.

The drive back to HQ takes forever, and I swear each light turns red as I approach.

"Why are there red lights in the middle of the night?" I shout at one, pounding the steering wheel. It's tempting to run them all, except the cameras would catch me. The bosses wouldn't be too happy at having to pay them off, assuming they aren't quantum angry at me for going against their orders.

Each time I stop, I peek in the rearview mirror at my hair. Between the bouts of feeling like a badass, I worry Drew might think it looks bad. I didn't do this for him, I did it for me, so why what he might think keeps popping up in my mind is a mystery. It doesn't matter what he thinks, and if he hates it, well that's too damn bad.

After too long of a drive I pull into the garage, park my SUV, and gallop over to the elevator. Safiya isn't here yet, so I adopt a casual pose and pretend I've been waiting like it's no big deal. She shows up a couple of moments later, and we enter the elevator together without saying anything.

She's also in all black but has kept her hair. Coward.

The doors ding, and we step out, neither one of us trying to go first or anything like that. She's a bit stronger, but I'm taller with better leverage, so I end up in front. Omari is still in charge at this hour, so I shouldn't have to explain anything to him about what's going on. He should be able to figure it out.

"Hey there, ladies," he purrs as we walk through the door, leaning against a locker. "What can I do you for tonight?"

He's got his squad in full gear and cleaning their weapons, having no doubt given them some excuse about training or being prepared or something, it doesn't matter.

"Here for a random inspection," I say, emphasizing the last words and giving him a pointed look that says, "*Two* trips to Sakura." "Why don't you clear everyone out of here so we can get to work?"

"Right away, your highness," he drawls, herding his squad out of the room and shooting me a question with his eyebrows. I shake my head and he responds with a shrug and a wink.

Alone in the armory, we equip ourselves as if we're professionals at this sort of thing. There're no words exchanged, only the sound of metal and zippers and boots and buckles.

This is supposed to be a covert action, not a full-out assault, so I take and load a couple of handguns. I'd prefer not to use a gun if I have a choice, but our enemies won't have any compunction about it. If I shoot a few people in the legs, they'll survive. They aren't fragile like humans. If we charge in with automatics, spraying bullets everywhere, we won't get far, and if we get stuck in a spot where we'd need that much firepower, there's no way we're getting out. Safiya seems to agree with my mental assessment, since she's also equipped a light loadout.

If this were a movie, there would be some intense music playing over the whole scene. Grim faces, tension running through the air, decisive movements. No hesitation. Doing what needs to be done. Instead, my hands are shaking, and my antiperspirant is working in overdrive. Regulating my breathing is important: deep and steady breaths in and out.

This is crazy, which is why I have to do it.

Drew would do it for me.

Did it for me.

I'm delaying on purpose. I need to get over this fear. It's not like I haven't gone out into the field before, but I wasn't the lead or in charge of the assaults. Any time I went, it was more as an observer, an overseer, someone the head honchos sent along to lend an air of gravity to important missions. I've had the required range training, I can handle a weapon, but using it on real people isn't something that happens all that often.

Of course, I also don't often take a bite out of someone's neck, and it's happened twice in two days. Before getting caught up in Drew, it had been years since I'd been forced to defend myself that way. Each one is a nasty memory. None of them makes me feel good, and I wish all of them hadn't happened. Except maybe for the one against the dragon, which distracted it long enough to keep it from killing Drew.

"You ready?" Safiya asks, breaking into my thoughts.

I blow out a heavy breath. "Yeah. Yeah, let's go. I'm driving." I snag the key fob for one of our vans on the way out. No need to risk damage to my vehicle.

Safiya mutters something under her breath, but I sweep past her and march toward the van, feeling bulky and heavy in all the armor. I wish I had tough skin like some other specials, or the crazy-strong bones Drew has. My healing is helpful, but it doesn't mean things don't hurt like a bitch or won't kill me super easy. Healing only helps after the battle, not during it.

As I depress the fob, the van beeps, and the satisfying pop as the door slides open makes me aware of how everything is heightened by adrenaline. My senses are in overdrive as adrenaline starts to flood my body, anticipating the coming conflict.

The seat is not comfortable, made less so by the armor and straps and weapons, and as I lean over to open the passenger door something pinches my side. How anyone does anything with all this stuff attached to them is beyond me.

"Drive," she says, gesturing, as if I'm sitting around and doing nothing.

"I'm going," I attempt to say without the inflection of irritation I've been holding back for hours. The engine turns over and we're off.

"I can't believe they've been so close this whole time and we never found out, but they knew where we were."

"A better question is, why didn't Lindberg tell you?" It's something that's been bothering me for some time, ever since I found out who he really is.

"I don't know. That's something I'd like to know too. No matter how many times I asked, he wouldn't tell me."

"Did he give a reason?" I slide my eyes over to her while paying attention to the road. While it's still the middle of the night, daybreak is coming, and the traffic isn't as dead as it was when I got home.

"He kept saying we weren't ready to know yet. He didn't want us launching before we could handle it."

"Hm." All of that was mentioned in the official transcripts, of course, but it's still good to hear some things direct from the source. It's a way to judge if it's credible. Transcripts won't tell you if the person asking the question was doing it as a standard course of action because they needed to or because they were trying to find out a real answer. Her tone suggests she was trying to get answers.

"Which is a ridiculous reason, of course," she continues, alternating between watching out the front window and the side. "I couldn't get him to give it up, even with all the pressure HQ wanted me to apply."

"He's got other motives." Which is worrying. Being undercover means you can keep secrets, and there's no guarantee we'll ever know what all his secrets are. He could be doing all this for his own gain. Perhaps he'll get us to eliminate Costecu, and then take over himself, getting rid of whoever comes after him in the process.

Using me, and us, to destroy strong enemies who might oppose his power grab would be a smart thing to do. Costecu, Gil, Jackson. We could be driving straight into a trap. His shouted words at me to rescue him the bait, and me the willing fish.

Remembrances of his searing gaze with only the glass between us, and after when he'd yanked off my towel, exposing me to him, dance through my mind. There's no way any of that was fake unless he's a hell of an actor. It doesn't mean my newfound fears can't be true, but it makes me hope they aren't. There's no way someone who looks at another person like that could be evil at heart. Right?

I loosen my grip on the steering wheel as my hands start to hurt. I won't let myself think that way. I'll rescue him. We'll rescue him, and then I'll find out what the perfectly reasonable reason was for keeping Costecu's base location a secret. Then I'll understand and have no reason not to trust him. You can't have a relationship without trust.

Safiya's said something to me.

"What?"

"I said, are you okay? You look a bit paler than normal."

"Yeah. It's a stressful situation, you know?" I squeeze and release the steering wheel some more, the worn rubber rubbing off on my palms.

"A little, sure. We'll succeed."

I can't tell if she's downplaying it to seem tough, or if it doesn't bother her much. She doesn't have any more field experience than I do, so there's no reason she should be more confident. She *is* one of those annoying stubborn people who always think they're right and can't fail in anything they do. From my understanding, a lot of men at gyms and bars find that attractive, as if that translates into confidence.

She's nowhere near the same as Drew. He's confident, not arrogant. He gets done what he says he's going to get done. It's not even close to the same thing at all. Confidence is hot. Drew is hot, therefore he's confident, not arrogant.

Safi is arrogant, but she has the swagger to pull it off half the time, and more so around those star-struck guys who fall into her fiery path.

This isn't good. Now's not the time to get stuck in my head debating whether Drew is a triple agent, or arrogant, or who the fuck knows what else. I can't have any doubts about this, or I'm going to get myself killed. I know that much. There can't be any hesitation, everything has to be decisive.

As we leave the highway and head into the industrial area, I divert my mind into more enjoyable things. Puppies, kittens, rainbows, thunderstorms, being naked in a thunderstorm, being naked in a thunderstorm while Drew makes love to me. Being naked in a thunderstorm while Drew makes love to me and feeds me chocolate at the same time.

After imagining all of the sexiness, relaxed isn't the word I'd use to describe my state of mind, but at least I'm no longer stressed. I really want him to feed me chocolate.

"We'll park here," I say, noting the familiar surroundings. This is where Drew parked us the first time, after he'd abducted me. It's perhaps a bit risky to be in the same spot, but the urge to relive those memories, though they're only a few days old, is strong.

Climbing out and walking down the sidewalk triggers all sorts of feelings. Here's where he confronted those thugs and ran them off with words alone. This is where he steadied me when I tripped over the huge crack. Next to that overpass pillar is where he pinched my ass when I kept mouthing off to him.

With the benefit of hindsight, it's clear as day how much I wanted him, and yet how much I was denying it to myself. I'm not sure what about him is driving this need, besides his competence, confidence, humongous muscles, and the whole thing where he killed a dragon almost single-handedly to keep me safe. Those reasons seem like good guesses as to why my insides are in a warm twist.

He might've had sex with Safiya, but I'd bet my life he didn't kill a dragon for her. That's got to be a first. I'm sure he has needs. It's okay that he had sex with her.

He had better sex with me.

Then we're at the steel door I recognize all too well. Beyond it was the first time I met the frightening Gil, and after that the elevator, Costecu, and torture. Extra nerves I didn't realize I had flutter up into my stomach, as flash after flash of all the pain I endured blast through my mind.

Safiya shakes my shoulder. "You okay?" she whispers.

"Yeah." I step back a few paces, taking her with me, away from the door, in case someone is watching or listening.

"What should we expect? Talk me through it live."

I take a deep breath. "I don't know. Gil the dragon was guarding this door. He's dead. They must have someone up here, but who?"

"I doubt it's unguarded."

I think about that for a moment or two. "It might be. Costecu's got Lindberg. From my few interactions with him, he's about the flashy things, the in-the-moment things. Costecu is about fashion, presenting as impressive even if it means sacrificing practicality. I got the impression Lindberg ran the day-to-day stuff and Costecu was concerned with the big picture. He might not think about sending someone up here. Might be too busy torturing Lindberg."

"Well, I guess there's only one way to find out," she says, then steps around me, pulls out a gun, grabs the door handle, and opens the door.

I'd like to say I don't squish back against the wall and wait to see if she gets bitten in half by something, but that's exactly what I do. Nothing happens, and she slips inside.

I shake myself loose and follow her into the den of our enemies, determined to be the first person Drew sees.

CHAPTER SIXTEEN

Aideen

The room beyond the door is silent, no sign of anything to indicate a guard might've gone off to the bathroom. No book, no phone, no coffee, and nothing that smells like a bored person waiting for nothing to happen.

Quietly, I shut the door to the outside, leaving us in dim lighting, and turn to Safiya. "No one's here. Lucky," I whisper.

She's poking around the nook where Gil must've spent most of his days. "So, you said he was here, watching the door? No locks or anything?"

"Yeah. We opened the door and walked in, no locks. I don't think anyone was going to get past him without a lot of trouble."

"Hm."

I move next to her to find her studying a large black button on the wall. There's no lettering and not much sign of wear. "Maybe a panic button?"

"Probably. Should leave it alone. Is there anything else up here?"

"Not that I know of. Only the other room with the elevator."

"We should look anyway?"

We split off heading in opposite directions. It's like I remembered it: a small room with an opening into what I'm starting to think of as the lobby. On one wall there's a clear sign of what used to be another doorway, but it's been filled in and covered up. The floor, a dirty mosaic of linoleum tiles, is accented by dim lighting. Overall, there's a feeling of an abandoned school or medical ward.

We meet up at the elevator doors. "This is the only way down?" she asks.

"Unless you found a secret staircase over there."

"No need to be snarky."

I bite back a snarky reply. "We could push the button, but that wouldn't be too smart. It opens right into the main area."

"How far down is it?"

"A handful of floors?"

"Can we get these doors open?" She tries to get her fingers in the gap between the double doors.

"These things are mechanically locked. Unless we had the tool that goes in there," I point to the little hole the key would go in, "we don't stand a chance of opening it."

"They do it in movies all the time," she complains, unable to get purchase in the gap to use the strength djinn have to pry it open.

"This isn't movies." I bet Drew could get it open with one hand.

"Shit. Then we're going to need to find another way."

I glance at the floor. "Guess we need to go...down."

"What?" She glances at the floor then back at me. "Oh, no. Heck no. C'mon. No."

"It's the best option I've got, unless you can think of anything else."

"You know what that does to me. There's got to be another way." She starts to pace the room, leans in to feel the walls, exam the cracks, and then taps her feet.

"You know I don't like it either. It makes me throw up."

"Damn it, Aideen. Maybe we can cut through the floor?"

"With what?" I'm not happy with what I'm suggesting, but I'm telling the truth. I don't see any other way around it. The elevator is far too obvious, and it will cut short our operation the moment the doors open to Costecu's central hub. There's no reason to believe our luck will continue if we keep pushing it.

"Ugh. Fuck. Ugh." She slaps the wall, making another circuit, poking her head back into the alcove by the door again. After a few more minutes of pacing, while I stand in the middle of the room waiting, she throws her hands up. "Fine."

"You'll want to aim about ten feet that way," I say, turning toward the elevator doors and pointing at an angle to my right.

"That's not good enough. 'About' isn't going to cut it. You need to get a lot more specific. How far down is it? For real."

I sigh and try to remember how many floors are between here and the central hub. I have no idea how fast the elevator was going, but it's old, and didn't feel all that rapid. I compare it to our elevators in our offices where it takes twenty seconds to go eleven floors. This old thing took only about ten seconds, and seemed a lot slower. So, four floors, maybe nine feet per floor, that's thirty-six feet. Shaving off a little since I'd rather have to drop down than end up embedded in stone, gives me thirty-three feet.

"Let's say thirty-three feet down and ten feet that way, then another three that way. Should put us away from the entrance and in a side room."

"Or in solid rock."

"Yeah, well, don't go into solid rock."

"You know it doesn't work that way," she grumbles before grabbing my hand. "Close your eyes. Not that it'll help much."

When a djinn teleports somewhere, multiple things happen. Their eyes tend to glow, or perhaps their skin takes on a slight luminescence. It's a function of doing what someone desires them to do, which is ingrained in their bones, but also makes them crabby. I've seen flames burst from the top of a djinn's head once when he was forced to do something very much against his will.

I close my eyes, because it does help block out the sight of things changing and twisting in the rapid fashion that happens when Safiya teleports. Air still rushes over what skin is exposed, raising the fine hairs along my arms, and then with what I can only describe as a popping feeling, everything slams to a halt.

We tumble a couple feet to the floor. The nausea overcomes me before I can gather any sort of sense, and I fall to my hands and knees and retch.

"You're going to get us caught," Safiya hisses from somewhere nearby. She's impatient, tugging at my arm and trying to get me to stand up.

"Shut up, shut up," I mutter, trying to pull away as the dizziness keeps swimming through my head. I heave again, my stomach attempting to empty anything that might be left inside. The last thing I ate was yogurt back in my condo, and before that it was a bag of chips. Perhaps not healthy living, but at least there's not a lot to evacuate.

"At least move to the side." She shoves me with her hip until I bump against the wall. The darkness is resolving into shapes, but since I'm looking down, the only thing in focus is the floor and splashed bits of yogurt.

"You always get so demanding," I say, wiping my mouth on my sleeve and spitting to try to get rid of the rest of the acid. It's normal for djinn to get a lot less diplomatic the more they use their powers. Something to do with being a creature of fire and explosive personalities.

"You wanted it, so too bad."

"Ugh." I stand and lean against the wall, taking deep breaths to try to get my nausea under control. The teleportation process always leaves me off balance. Something about brain chemicals and being zapped across space occupied by other stuff without interacting with any of it tends to throw my brain for a loop.

Safiya stands in front of me, her hands on her hips, her eyes glowing orange. I snicker.

"What?"

"Headlights."

"Shut up."

"Make sure you signal when you turn."

The orange light dims as she narrows her eyes. "Why don't you get it together so we can stop standing out in the open?"

"Sorry. You're right."

Whoosh. In a flash we've moved to another room.

"Sorry. Okay. I'm good."

"Fine. Which way?"

"Uh. Out the door and to the right if we're going to the dungeons, which should be our first stop. We should probably keep talking to a minimum from here on out."

"No shit," she says, tugging on some of the armor's straps. "This crap is too tight."

"Huh?"

"Body transformation, don't worry about it. Go, let's go. Lead. Start."

"Fine, fine."

I crack open the door and peek through the slit before pulling it all the way to survey the hallway beyond. No one's there. We must've been unnoticed. In fact, it's pretty quiet. Whether that's good or bad is yet to be determined.

I crouch, motion all clear, and sneak out of the door. If I get nothing else out of this, it'll be a good thigh workout. It's stupid, but if I let myself get too serious, I'll freak out, and that wouldn't be good for anyone. What would Drew do? March through the halls and punch the head off of anyone who got near, which is not an option, but I can do the same thing in spirit.

One of the guns is in my hands and my talisman feels like a tiny star against my sternum. I can smell Safiya behind me, a slight whiff of ozone and flame. I've only seen her go full djinn once, and it was impressive and terrifying. The orange eyes are only the tip of the iceberg.

Step by careful step, we make our way down the dark hallways. The occasional shout or echoing of footsteps comes from down other hallways, and each time we pause and hover in whatever nook or doorway is nearby until the sounds fade. Our luck can't hold out forever.

As if the universe is listening, someone comes around the corner. Before they can react, I launch forward and grab them around the knees, driving with my legs until we crash into the wall on the other side. Besides not getting myself killed, the main objective will be to shut this person up before they start shouting. A bright flash comes over me, washing out my sight and making dots dance in my vision. Then the shout of alarm I was afraid of bubbles off to nothing.

I scoot back away from a burst of heat in front of me, blinking to get my night vision back, but it turns out I don't need it. Safiya is over me, her legs straddling us, her hand around the throat of the enemy, flames licking out from between her fingers. The bubbling sound is the air escaping from his deceased body.

She's seared through his skin and muscles in a second, and when she releases her grip, his head flops at a crazy angle, halfway off his body. The burn marks from her fingers char what's left of the skin. The white-hot flames disappear, leaving a bright spot in the middle of my vision.

I roll over onto my back and scoot out the rest of the way. She drops to one knee beside the body, breathing hard.

"You okay?" I whisper.

"Yeah. Give me a second."

I watch her as I get up and stand. Her face is hidden as she kneels next to the body, bracing one hand on the floor. As my night vision comes back, there are a few clear singed spots in the places of her clothing not covered by armor.

She's told me it's exhausting to go full-form and maintain it for any length of time, unless it's in direct response to someone she cares for asking. According to common knowledge about djinns, if they ever get seriously involved with someone as in deep in love, that person has a fair amount of control over them. Most djinns end up in a long series of casual relationships because they fear giving up that much control. Safiya is not any different. A few times, after many drinks, she's told me how lonely she is.

I keep watch in case anyone else was nearby and saw the flash of flame or heard the disturbance. But no one shows up. I count to sixty.

"Sorry to do this, but we need to get rid of the body and move," I say, reaching to put a hand on her shoulder. It's still warm.

"Yeah. Okay."

I help her up, and then we drag the body into a side room and stuff it behind some storage racks. By the time anyone smells it, we should be out of here for good, or dead. The flames cauterized the wound before any blood could drip out or leave a trail, and the victim was a vamp, so we got lucky to not run into a flame-retardant species.

We wait for her eyes turn from hot embers to cool coals, then we sneak out and finish our trip to the dungeons. Along the way, there are clear signs of conflict. The mess strewn about makes it obvious people have lost their lives. There are bodies kicked into corners and wet, dark stains splashed against surfaces. Discolored splotches appear in random places on the wall and floor, getting more frequent as we get closer to the cells.

"Lindberg?" Safiya asks in my ear, her breath furnace hot.

I wouldn't be surprised he had something to do with this mess, but there's no way to know. We round the final bend to the cell block, and I pull up short. All the doors are open or ajar, there are bodies scattered across the floor, and none of the groaning and moaning I remember hearing during my incarceration here is present.

The place is empty.

"What the hell?"

"Lindberg definitely happened to this."

I straighten and step down the hall, avoiding the gruesome leftovers of whatever battle took place. There's a tense moment when I reach the cell where I'd been interred, and my stomach turns over. The lighting isn't as dim as I remember, but when Safiya moves behind me and casts a faint glow emanating from her eyes into the crevasses of the room, that mystery is explained.

"Anything in there?" she asks from behind me.

"No. Nothing." I turn away, not willing or able to relive any of those nasty memories.

A quick search shows all the other cells as empty as mine, not one person inside them, or any signs of life. The only thing I can think, the only thing I want to think, is Drew broke out and freed everyone to cover his escape. Then why didn't we meet him on the way, or why didn't he show up at HQ? It's not comforting to imagine we might have missed him by minutes, and all this is for nothing.

"They've been here a few hours," Safiya says, toeing one of the bodies. "It's not fresh. See, the blood is all dried?"

"Yeah." I pace a few steps. "Then we go to the interrogation room. If he did this, and didn't get out, then Costecu would have him, and I imagine he's pretty pissed."

"I agree," she says, shrugging. "Lead the way."

My thighs and butt are not happy about the prospect of tactical crouching the whole way there, so I opt to go slower than before. With Safiya's eyes still crackling like embers, we're liable to get caught at any moment, so stealth is perhaps not as effective as it was to start. As empty as the lair has been, maybe it won't matter, and we'd have the potential riot in the cell block to thank for that.

The corridors are as empty as before. Perhaps the living areas are more crowded. Tracing my steps back to the room I was tortured in, the knot in my stomach turns into a massive cinder block. My toe throbs in sympathetic memory, and an imaginary ache in my pinky starts pinging. We make it to the interrogation room without further incident, which is good, but also worrying. Where is everyone?

"This is, um, where I was," I say as I stare into the depths of the room. The steel shutter is up and the hated chair where I was strapped is sitting in the middle of the room like a monstrous monument to malice. There's no sign of Drew.

"Are there others?"

"I don't know. Let's look."

There are others, four others, a total of five rooms stuffed with pain, anguish, and death. What a horrible way to exist, and a terrible place to have your life end. The last one has a body, limp and dead. The bruising around his neck, swollen tongue, and broken blood vessels in his eyes indicate strangulation. Not a pleasant way to go out at all.

"Still a little warm," Safiya says, her hand on the corpse's neck.

"Shit. Do you think... Those are big handprints." My stomach churns.

She closes the corpse's eyes. "Where to next?"

I'm glad to dismiss that line of thought. "I guess we head to the...throne room. We have to check."

I turn around and almost slam into someone huge, muscular, and solid as a rock.

"Drew," Safiya shouts in surprise, sending me rocking between my own surprise and large amounts of disgust. *Drew? First name basis? The fuck?*

I take a step back, intending to greet him in a way I usually talk to him, but the words die in my throat. It's *Drew* all right, the whole entire uninjured body of him, but his eyes are wrong. They're all wrong. He's all wrong.

A huge meaty hand swings out and smashes me aside. My scream is cut off when I crunch into the rock wall and black out.

CHAPTER SEVENTEEN

Druain

After what might be hours or days of running, always ending up back at the dirt road entrance to my cabin, the last few circuits have been ridiculous.

I'm still in tune with what's happening outside the prison of my mind. I've left the dead body of the person I killed behind, and I'm following Costecu somewhere. It's like wearing ten layers of clothes. I can sort of feel what's going on, but everything is muffled and slow.

This is fucking stupid, I project at imaginary Zero, not bothering wasting theoretical breath when I don't need to speak out loud.

So fix it.

What?

Fix it. This is your brain. Stop being stupid.

I glance over to see her hair whipping in the wind, her face determined and flushed from the exertion, fit and hot, and amazing.

Shit, I need to get out of here pronto so I can see her for real. See her and touch her.

Okay, genius, what should I do?

You're asking me for advice? If I had to tell you what to do, I'd be disappointed. Figure it out.

I keep staring at her while thinking and running. Because I can. It's my brain. I can do what I want. It's always been my brain, and I can always do what I want. This banshee is twisting me up so much I'm forgetting this is my world and she's the invader.

I stop running, as does Zero.

What are you doing?" she turns to me and yells.

Hush, Zero. Trust me."

She crosses her arms and glares. The first time she does that when I get out of here I'm going to grab those arms, pin them over her head, and kiss her until she's drunk and dizzy.

I look away so I can concentrate. Since it seems I need to get to the scene of the crash to get out of here, all I need to do is be there. I don't need to run, or walk, or move. I can just...be there.

Everything slams to a halt, then the scenery sucks itself into a hole in the middle of my vision before bouncing back like goo, right to where I want to be. There's the SUV on its side, Costecu's vehicles and men are there, and everything is frozen in time.

"There, see? We're here."

"After I had to give you a pep talk," Zero says, rolling her eyes before sidling forward to investigate, her gun out, the perfect picture of cautious curiosity.

No one moves. It's as still as stone.

Memory me is there, out of the SUV and facing Costecu, emerging from the cocoon of his own SUV. All the creatures he'd brought with him are staggered between us, most concentrating on me. Zero is sheltering behind me, glaring at Costecu like she wants to light him on fire. It's a perfect tableau of silence in the moments before it all went crazy.

I scan for the banshee, but don't see her anywhere. As an experiment, I walk up to frozen and fake Costecu and punch him in the face. It's like punching a mountain.

"Ow, motherfucker, fuck."

"Idiot," Zero snickers.

"Shut up. That jaw is like granite."

"Duh. Time is stopped. You can't move anything until time starts again. Something about thermodynamics or whatever."

"I guess I know more than I realized," I say, weaving through the scene, stuck in time like a butterfly on a pinboard. "What am I supposed to do now, smarty-pants?"

Zero shrugs. "Beats me. You wanted to come here." She pops herself up onto the hood of one of the SUVs and crosses one leg over the other, watching me, looking hot, as always.

"I can work under duress. You could be naked and—" Then she's naked for a hot second, seizing up my thought processes until I forcibly imagine the hiking clothes for her again. "God damn it. Don't do that."

She pretends to study her fingernails.

"I'm going to talk through the problem," I say. "It'll help me. You don't have to answer."

"Because you're slow?"

"Zero, if this wasn't a life-or-death situation, you'd be in so much trouble. In fact, you're only making it worse for your real self when I get out. Now quiet. Let me think."

The heat of her gaze follows me as I pace up and down, weaving between people frozen in time.

"I can't get out there because the damn banshee has me all locked up. Except she's scared, because if I catch her, I'm going to tear her limbs off and then all her teeth out. So she's hiding."

Outside, the sky shows me and Costecu reaching his throne room. He sits on his chair, facing me. His voice sounds like listening to a tuba through syrup.

"Why did I come here?" I continue. "Because I thought I'd find her. It made sense. She's trying to show me horrible things to throw me off balance or something. Horrible things centered around you."

"So you think I'm horrible?"

I don't bother with imaginary banter. Costecu is still talking to me in real time. Something about his grand plans, and how he's going to use me to wreak havoc on his enemies. He says he's disappointed we couldn't work together, but with my brute strength, I can still do good for him. He's going to send me to storm Zero's headquarters and kill as many people as I can before they take me down.

I stop pacing and glare at his face, twisted and huge in the sky as he says he wants me to track down the woman he still calls Moarte, the woman I risked everything for, and kill her as slowly as possible. The head on top of my unresponsive body nods, and I spin to start beating on the SUV.

Instead of the pleasant crunch of metal, it's as hard as frozen Costecu's face. "Son of a bitch."

"Thermodynamics, remember?" Zero says, perched on the hood. "It affects everything."

I narrow my eyes. It doesn't matter here. Nothing does. Nothing is real. The only reality is out there.

I punch the vehicle a few more times. My hand starts to bleed, bones crack, but when I concentrate, everything heals back up to normal, letting me punch some more. The first time I understood I can do anything here should've been enough for the knowledge to sink in, but it's difficult to unlearn years of cause and effect as it applies to everything in the real world.

If this were a hedge maze, I could spend hours and days tracing every track, every passage, trying to figure out how to get from the entrance to the exit. The hedges could change, and the rules could bend. Instead of following the maze, why don't I go through it? Push through the walls themselves.

"Sorry, Zero. Time for you to go."

"Aw. We were having so much fun." She pouts, something the real Zero would never do. It makes it a bit easier to do what comes next.

"Yeah. I'll see you outside soon, and then we'll get to have all sorts of fun."

She smiles, and then her eyes go large as saucers and her mouth drops open as I shoot her in the head. Her body topples off of the SUV, lifeless and bloodless, and as it hits the pavement everything around me winks out.

Two points of light resolve in the distance and then rush at me, smashing together into one solid blob, a dizzying blend of colors and perspective, until it all turns into a view I wasn't expecting.

Costecu, staring at me, right at me, and asking a question.

"Are you all right, my dear? You look a bit pale. Ah, excuse me, paler than normal." He chuckles and it sets my teeth on edge.

What the hell is he talking about? Am I back in my body? Nothing feels connected, and it takes a great deal of concentration to raise what might be my hand. Except, as it levitates into sight, it's not my hand. It's pale, laced with blue veins, long and ragged nails, and thin skin. Shit. It's the banshee's hand.

Sickness grabs at my stomach and twists hard. I cough, and the banshee coughs out of the same lungs and same cracked mouth.

"Do you need a hanky?" Costecu asks, pulling one out of his pocket.

Fuck, shit, balls. I'm in the banshee's mind, controlling her body. What kind of twisted mental game is this? I can't see Zero like this. I don't have the equipment to have sex with her, and I can't protect her in this frail body.

Get me out of here, get me out.

My vision swoops to the side, and Costecu reaches out to catch me—the banshee—by the arm.

"Steady there, old girl."

His touch is like ants, lava, bamboo shoots, salt in a wound, wet socks in the morning. It's the worst feeling I've ever suffered through, and I want it to end. Lashing out with my right hand, I try to punch him. The delay between my desire and the action is massive, clumsy, and might as well be the time it takes for a glacier to carve a valley.

He stops the flail without blinking, and then tips his head to the side. "Is there something wrong, dear Sorcha? Do we need to adjourn to my office?"

I pull, yank, try anything to free my, her, whoever's, wrist from his grip, but it's like steel, and banshees aren't physically strong. I might as well be buried in concrete.

"Lllaaaeeet mmmeer goooeeerr." The voice speaking is strange and not mine. It's slow, slurring, lips move like bumper cars in a hurricane, and I've got no clue how to control her vocal cords when I've got to focus on using them. No wonder it takes babies a whole year to learn to talk.

"Hm?"

"Fffuuuook yyoouu."

"That's not very civil," Costecu says, eyes narrowing. "Are you having a stroke?"

"Grrrrr. Gooonnaa...geeetchhuuu..." I can't stand being this near to him while having no power to snap his neck.

He drags me—the banshee—over to a chair and shoves her down, leaning so close I can smell his breath, stale and moist like moss. "You're going to...get me?"

I've got a handle on the controls, at least enough it's no longer like moving through syrup. I'm not sure what's going to happen when he kills the banshee, but I'm going to make sure it happens. I'm not going to spend any longer in this rotten shell than I have to.

Maybe it'll kill me, maybe I'll snap back, and maybe I'll end up some vengeful spirit, but the thing I'm not going to do is go out without a fight.

"Gooot herr. 'M iinnn herr. Thisss iis miinne nnow. Fuuck yoouuu."

He frowns and grabs the banshee's chin, holding her face steady while he keeps peering at her, almost as if he's looking past her at whatever part of me is inside her mind.

I start to struggle. It's pathetic, how weak this body is. I couldn't come close to doing any physical harm to Costecu, but maybe I can do something with whatever she's got in her head. He's ancient and must be somewhat immune to her wail, but it can't hurt to try.

It's all in the note. That specific note she hits that's not anything normal people can make. Something that bridges the gap between reality and fantasy. Then there's the worming in the brain thing. I'm not sure how to do that, but I try anyway.

The only note I can produce is a creaky and off-tune buzz, not able to hold the same pitch or volume for more than a few seconds. I've never been much of a singer. Costecu seems half-amused and half-angry, so while he's deciding what to do, I poke his brain.

I'm thrown back in shock as my mental finger is flung aside by cold iron and colder steel. Costecu blinks.

"That was odd. Are you trying to use your power against me?"

Knowing I'll fail, I try again so he can't be mistaken. It's the same thing as before, all corners and hard metal and corridors with nothing in them but fog. I get further this time. "Fuck you," I crackle-sing. I won't stop trying until I can't anymore.

He blinks twice then, until his mouth curls into a sneer. "Trying to 'renegotiate' our deal? I wouldn't do that again if you know what's good for you."

What a dumbass. "Donn't get it? Shee's gone. It's me, ffucker. Gonnna kill you." I poke his brain again and have a good two seconds of studying all the doors along the corridor before I'm tossed out harder than before. If I had any practice or knowledge of how to do this, I bet I could put him in the ground. I beat the banshee, and they're supposed to be tough.

"You? Who is you?" he asks, but by the clench of his jaw and the coldness in his eyes, he knows the answer.

"Goona rip youur heaad offff," I shout in a rising note, and right at the end it bursts into a glorious chime, the perfect tone, no doubt nothing to do with me and everything to do with muscle memory.

I poke at him again, see the flash of the hallway, and run at one of the doors. Right as I hit it, barreling through and revealing the contents of the room beyond, something swoops in and grabs me.

Talons of pure ice, the type that burns and freezes, grip my shoulders and fling. A screech hundreds of times worse than Gil's shatters the air, and I'm back in the banshee's body in time for Costecu to grab her head and snap her neck.

It's a sickening feeling, to have your neck broken. I've done it enough times to know the sound, but this is the first time I've felt it happen from the other side. There's a split-second to register what's going on, and then I'm turned inside out and shot through the air like a bullet from a gun.

Everything goes dark, then white, then red, then upside down, and then I'm staring at Safiya's frightened face.

CHAPTER EIGHTEEN

Aideen

A bright star against my chest wakes me up, leeching the blackness out from behind my eyes leaving a searing brightness. I open my eyes to get away from the light behind my lids, which leaves me with the darkness of Costecu's' bolt-hole along with a swimming headache. I paw at the talisman beneath my shirt, the star that's burning my skin, and only then register what happened.

"Lindberg," I gasp as air rushes back into my burning lungs and the bulk of the man who hit me looms to the side. "What the hell?"

He's not looking at me, and he's not speaking to me when he says, "Safi?"

"Drew. Are you okay?" Safiya is backed into the corner of the room, putting the chair with the corpse between her and Drew.

"What are you doing here?" He sounds puzzled and disoriented, which scares me. He's never sounded unsure. His clothing is ragged, his face bruised, his fingers stained with what I'll pretend is cranberry juice.

My knees are uncooperative and wobbling so I drag myself up by some chained instruments then smack him in the back of his shoulder. "Hey. Idiot."

He whips around and almost backhands me again, pulling up a couple of inches from my face, a swirl of air kissing my cheeks. "Zero?"

"What?" Safiya asks.

I hadn't told her that part. It's a silly nickname. Not relevant. "Why'd you hit me?"

"I hit you? What are you... You're here? You cut your hair."

"Do you like it?" I cringe inside. Not the time. "I mean, of course I'm here, you thi—"

"Ah," a voice whispers through the air like a knife. "My two favorite people, and a new guest."

As one, we spin to the source. Costecu is standing in the doorway, smiling in the politest way possible, a grotesque creature posing as a gentleman.

"Oh, shit," Safiya says, and then Drew rushes him. In the space of a blink, he's up against the wall, face to the stone, with Costecu's grip around his arm and shoulder.

"Now, now. Let's not be rude," Costecu sing-songs, and I nod my head. "I'm sure we can all come to an agreement about how you'll die."

"Drew, listen to him," Safiya says.

She needs to stop doing that. Stop calling him Drew, and stop telling him what to do. "Don't do that," I say, then grab at my head as a spike of pain rolls through it, knocking me to my knees.

"Zero."

"Don't be unreasonable, just do it," Safiya shouts, a tone of panic rising in her voice as she comes into the middle of the room.

I'm torn between agreeing, because Costecu is right, but no one should tell Drew what to do. He's always done the right thing when it comes to me. My mouth opens, but the pain hits me again and I flop to the floor.

"Ah, we have a tough one here," Costecu says, turning his attention to me and smiling, bright and beautiful.

"Fight it, Zero, fuck," Drew shouts and growls. "He's charming you, fight it."

Yes, he's quite charming. I can see why he's gotten so far. The only thing is, Drew is charming, too in his way. Protective, tough, confident, sacrificing himself to help me. So why are they fighting? They should be on the same side. Drew should be the one in charge.

The flash of pain this time is met by a zing from the talisman around my neck, and a scream is forced out from my throat, painting my vision red.

"Zero, look out."

Something hot lands on me, burning at my face while the smell of fire assaults my nostrils. I flail with my hands and latch onto an arm, a face. A person appears out of the red mist, a person with flaming orange eyes and hairline cracks across their skin, glowing from within.

"Well, won't this be enjoyable? Would you like to see your girlfriend torn to shreds?" Costecu laughs. "Don't have any mercy on her, my delightful djinn."

Drew shouts something, but by then I'm too busy fighting to keep Safiya's hands off of my throat. She's strong, too strong, stronger than I am, and there's nothing I can do.

The talisman pulses. As much as I don't want this option, I've got no other choice. Costecu could use it against me, anyone could yank it from me and use it, but if I die in the next five minutes it's not going to matter anyway.

Accepting the reality of it is all that's needed. A blinding tingle moves through me like an orgasm times ten. As long as she doesn't kill me in the three seconds it takes for the buzzing and dizziness to fade, I should be good. I should've done this before I was on the edge of death, but it's always been a last resort. It's not who I am.

Things get fuzzy as I grab her wrists and the selkie takes over, stretching and barking in excitement. My teeth snap as I try to bite her arms and my legs come up to wrap around her waist and squeeze. The burning subsides a little, soothed away as my skin thickens and oozes a thin protective coating.

Sounds of a struggle echo against the walls. Drew cursing like I've never heard before while Safi digs her thumbs into the soft flesh of my throat. The boom as the door slams open barely registers.

"Get him, get him," Costecu shouts to the menagerie of creatures who've appeared to help. Vampires are good in short bursts, but any fight lasting more than a couple of minutes leaves them drained. Drew grabs for him as he slinks off, but the mass of new bodies shoves him away.

I start winning the tug of war at my neck, loosening Safi's grip, letting me get some breath into my burning lungs. The air is acrid, filled with embers and the taste of charcoal.

"Stop," she growls in my face. "He's right, stop fighting."

I'm doing the right thing. I know I am. If it hurts, it's not what Costecu wants me to do. He's a vampire who's trying to kill us.

Someone flies over my head, and then Safiya is wrenched from me, dragging her nails across my neck as she's forced to let go.

"Get up, Zero," Drew urges, holding Safiya at the end of his arm. I don't need to be told twice.

Costecu's voice in my head is trying to tell me that it doesn't matter what happens to me. The bright burning pain each time I so much as consider fighting his control is pushed back by the waves coming from my talisman. I need to get Drew out of here.

So many conflicting thoughts stream through my brain, a pulse of good and bad, and it's too much to handle. I clap my hands to my temples and grit my teeth. Only one thing matters: keep Drew safe. With a howl, I launch myself at the nearest person, heedless of who or what they are, needing only to take them out.

My teeth latch on and my jaw works, and a scream erupts from near my ear. I taste blood, and yank my jaw back, tearing out a chunk of flesh, spitting it to the floor and dropping, ready to move on to the next. If the bleeding doesn't kill them, the poison will.

Another and another, I bite, chew, scratch, and attack. I have no idea if anyone is going down, content to wound if that's it what it takes to slow them down, to protect Drew. To get us out of here.

Costecu's orders are fading from my brain. I whip my head around to spot him slipping from the room. He's going to escape, run away, disappear, never to be punished for all he's done. Not a chance while I'm still up and fighting.

"Zero, be careful. Come back," Drew shouts, but I don't care. There are too many people between me and Costecu. I won't let him get away. A hulking creature with horns blocks my path, but launching off of the gurgling victim I'm leaving behind lands me around his shoulders.

He roars and grabs me around the waist, pulling hard, but I've got my teeth in his flesh and I'm not going to let go. My sightline is taken up by his neck and shoulder, muscles and sinews. A tendon snaps between my teeth as I chew and gnaw. A rib in my torso cracks as the minotaur squeezes and pulls. We spin until I'm crushed into the wall, knocking all the breath out of me and ripping my teeth loose from his skin, but not without taking a good chunk of it out.

He slams me against the wall again and again, rocking my vision back and forth in a jarring shudder of pain. My feet are nowhere near the ground, but that's not a problem in my current state of mind. Grabbing until I find purchase, and biting anything I can get my teeth on leads to many satisfying sounds of pain, but I can't last this way forever.

The minotaur jerks to the side and I tumble to the floor where I grab at his leg.

"Zero, fuck. Stop messing with this idiot," Drew yells. "He's going to come back, and we do *not* want to be here."

Safiya is wrapped around his back, arms around his neck, and how he managed to come over here and punch the minotaur is beyond me. She's a blazing inferno of heat and hell. The burning smell is Drew's flesh.

I grab the minotaur and give him another bite on the thigh, through his pants, spitting out another pound of flesh. Whatever charm Costecu had over me is gone with his distance, although why Safiya isn't back to normal I can't guess.

"Get her off," I shout.

"Trying," he says, backing into a wall at speed, eliciting an angry grunt from flaming Safiya. "Would rather not kill her."

A flash of anger heats my chest until I realize he must mean because she's a colleague, not because he's in love with her or anything.

He comes off the wall to shove me aside and breaks someone's nose behind me. "Stop gaping, Zero. Are you clearheaded?" I nod. "Then start punching or biting, or whatever you do. Get us an opening."

I push and shove, biting hands that get too close, shrugging off glancing blows thanks to my tough skin.

Growling, I hear a thud resonate behind me, and then two sharp slaps. I'd like to turn but I'm grappling with a vamp. He's trying to bite my neck while I try to bite his anything, and we're both trying to keep the other away. I get a hold of his wrist and crunch all the small bones in it with one chomp, headbutting him when he screams, and drop him to the floor.

"Time to go, Zero." Drew plows past me with an unconscious Safiya flaming out across his shoulders. He bowls into the mélange of monsters, scattering them like pins.

Then everyone is blown back into the room.

"Cover your eyes, don't look," he coughs out, but it's too late.

Costecu is in the doorway. He's glorious. Shining, bright, beautiful, handsome, smart, everything I could ever want in a man, woman, or person, standing in front of me like an angel from heaven and a devil from hell all bundled together.

"Kill him," he says, his voice like chimes, a piano, the culmination of every wonderful voice ever. He points a slender and perfect finger at Drew and my new purpose in life is clear.

End him forever.

CHAPTER NINETEEN

Druain

Costecu's blast of persuasion hits me hard, but my little adventure through my and the banshee's mind seems to have given me some sort of protection.

Instead of the charming and wonderful person everyone else sees him as, I can see his true nature. Blood smeared over his face from the massive infusion he must've drank to project this much power. His eyes are predatory, like a human-sized bird ready to swoop down on a rabbit miles below.

Zero doesn't look much better. The amount of blood and chunks she's got splattered across her face and chin is vampire levels of gross. I'm not sure if it's supposed to be that way, but the thick seal skin is unexpected, but not off-putting.

Seeing her almost in a frenzy, bouncing from thing to thing, taking on vampires, werewolves, going after a minotaur for fuck's sake, turns me on to levels I didn't know existed. Seeing Safi with her was a surprise since it'd been a few months since our last, and I had made clear final, "meeting."

Seeing her next to Zero swept away any final scraps of regret for having cut short what Safiya wanted to last forever. Zero is mine. And no one can compare.

Safi's turned to me with a nasty gleam in her eye, and Costecu's blood-drunk himself into the most powerful vamp I've seen yet.

The only thing I've got going for me is myself, and I'm in a bad state. I'm still not healed from the all the torture. My knees are not in top shape, and every muscle is throbbing, like someone's been wailing on them. Oh, yeah, they have been.

At least I've only got to deal with two opponents, and I only have to be careful with Zero. I won't be crying into my beer if I mess up Costecu's face. It's been the whole goal of this entire endeavor.

"Bring it on, tough guy," I say to Costecu, dropping into a crouch, which sets my legs aflame with pain. He laughs, a full-blown evil villain laugh, and then Zero rushes me.

I'd be lying if it wasn't one of the hottest things I've ever experienced. I've dreamed about something like this since I first saw her, but of course those dreams weren't in a lethal situation, and the fighting was for fun, not for my life. Still, seeing the intensity in her eyes and the determined set of her jaw is sexy beyond belief. One day we're going to recreate this, and instead of the end being me knocking her out, it's going to be us having crazy, passionate sex.

I grab her hair and spin as she comes flying in, swinging her around and knocking her into the wall, as carefully as one can bash someone into stone. She grunts, rebounds, and tries to jump on me, clawing at my forearm, both legs coming off the floor in an attempt to wrap around me and get closer. Close is the last thing I want to be to a snapping selkie, yet distance is the last thing I want to be with Zero. It feels odd holding her away, my arms straining as she hangs off of them.

Too late, I shift my attention to Costecu. He drives a punch into my kidney with the force of a barge. I topple to my knees, which allows Zero the opportunity to get her legs around me and squeeze.

"I was kinda hoping my first three-way would be with two women, but I guess this is okay," I wheeze as Costecu nails me in the other kidney.

He's past the point of words, a feral beast, the blood-frenzy having taken him.

I don't have a figurative seal skin like selkies do. I'm not able to turn into a vicious little beast, and I can't drink a gallon of blood and unleash the vampire within. I'm a dwarf. A son of stone. Tough, determined, and stubborn. All I've got is years of experience fighting monsters like this and staying alive. The secret is endurance. They'll both burn out so all I have to do is not lose until I win.

Still, it's easier said than done. My instincts are to duck and roll, putting Zero between me and Costecu. In a normal fight, I wouldn't give two shits if he shredded whatever other monster was dangling off me and used up half of his energy, but that's not an option. I won't do anything to get Zero injured. Not in a permanent way.

I duck, roll, and then roll more, using the weight of her hanging on my arms to clobber Costecu in the head before momentum taps her against the wall again. Not hard. A love tap. Maybe something will jar loose. Costecu's grunt after being blasted by a hundred and sixty-odd pounds of Zero is satisfying, but her grunt is less so.

"Sorry, Zero," I mumble, trying to poke her brain with mine. Nothing seems to happen. I guess dwarves don't have those abilities.

Her snarling face blinks and her eyes roll, but then she's right back at me, and catches the side of my face with her hand. It's a mighty wallop, and I see stars and gain more appreciation of my selkie. I spin again, this time tossing her right onto Costecu, who's rising from the floor, then follow after her.

Grabbing the back of her combat vest and yanking her off before he can do any damage, I kick him in the chin. If I can break him, the charm will fall, and Zero will be free. I need to keep her out of the fight for a few minutes.

I manage to get another kick in before she's on my back. The distraction of trying to peel her off gives Costecu the second he needs to rise like the dead. Anticipating his obvious move, I fling myself back and off my feet as he swipes at my head with claws of chitin and hit the floor.

The crack of bone breaking as Zero takes some of the fall is sickening, but most of the damage is to my elbows. The rush and thunder of the air going out of her lungs whooshes past my ear, and her grip disappears.

Stay down, Zero, please.

I brace. He's so much faster than any other creature I've ever encountered. By the time I've gotten a grip on his arm, his claws are embedded in my chest. I've been stabbed tons, so the feeling is not new, but it doesn't mean it feels good. His fingers are trapped between my dwarven ribs, and he can't rake or rip.

I roll off Zero, taking this asshole vamp with me. He's quick to react, but with the angle of his claws, and my hands locked around his arm, he's not quick enough. The full weight of my body comes down on his forearm, and the snapping of bones is music to my ears. I keep rolling like an alligator clamped on prey, until I've destroyed his arm and dragged him underneath me.

Zero is lying on the floor to my left, limp and smooshed, out cold. She's breathing. I can see the shallow movement of her chest. A weight lifts from mine, and I feel better.

Costecu is thrashing under me. I jab a palm into whatever part of him I can. Then he gets a grip and shoves hard forcing me up. I keep my grip on his arm and drag him with me as I tumble backward. The noises he makes are angry, but he fights.

He hits me in the side of the head, talons scratching at my face, searching for a hold. I twist around to face him moments before I'm blasted off my feet by a roiling ball of flame. Costecu goes flying in the other direction.

"Stop," Safi yells, pointing at me as I hit the ground and roll to put out the flames. "Leave him alone."

Great. Get one down and another one pops up like whack-a-moles. "Safi, he's charming you. Fight it, girl," I tell her in the firmest voice I can muster. Maybe that'll get through to her somehow. She always did like that.

Costecu chuckles, leaning against the wall and holding his arm. He's coming out of his frenzy, which would be the perfect moment to go after him, if Safi hadn't put herself between him and me.

"Don't you see how amazing he is?" she shrieks, burning tears running down her darkened face. "He's only trying to give us all the best world to live in."

Costecu is edging toward the door, no doubt to tap into his stash or maybe find some unsuspecting victims among his flock. He can't get away again.

"Sorry girl, I don't have time to argue with you right now." I go to push past her, but she grabs me and shoves me back, stronger than I remember her being. Of course, she never turned before.

"Don't let him leave this room, my little djinn," Costecu says, pausing in the doorway. "I'd be so disappointed in you."

"Don't worry. I won't," she says.

If I wasn't tired, exasperated, and beyond all of this shit, she might be fearsome. Black hair floating as if she's underwater, literal flames licking across her skin, dancing from her fingers, toes, and eyes. Did I mention she's naked because all of her clothes have burned away? Only some scraps of the body armor remain, hanging in charred shreds.

I try to get past her again, shoving first before she can push at me, attempting to barrel through and push past. She grabs me, her hands hot and burning, searing pain into my arm, but if a burn is the worst thing I get today, I'll be overjoyed.

"I don't want to hurt you," I tell her, grabbing her, ending up in some strange half-grapple position.

"Good. I don't want to hurt you either." I blow out a breath of relief, but then she continues. "Stay in here and let Costecu heal so he can come and kill you, and everything will be fine."

"Um, fuck no." I attempt a tuck and throw, but she reverses out of it, and then it's my turn to prevent the throw. She must practice them, and my height gives her an advantage in getting below my center of gravity.

We end up on the floor, rolling around in a tangle. She's quicker than Zero, a touch stronger, but a lot less thoughtful in her attacks, and less teeth, thank fuck. After a few fancy moves, I get her pinned under me. It's super distracting having a naked and literally hot woman under me. My body reacts in super inappropriate ways, as if I'm not in a fight for my life.

"This has been fantastic," I say, breathing heavy. "It's been a while since I've had a good wrestle, but I need to finish this. You're charmed, Safi. Nothing personal."

I move to put her into a headlock and knock her out, but in a flash her skin is so hot I can't hold onto her anymore. I try, and I last a few seconds before the heat is too much. Scrambling onto my knees, I wrap her hair in my fist to keep her down.

"Get off me. You won't stop him." she wails, and although I can't see her face, she sounds on the verge of tears.

"Ow, damn it, Safi, stop." The heat is intense, and I have no choice but to back off a step, and then another as she stands up and rotates to face me. It's such a smooth movement, and only then do I notice her feet aren't on the floor. They're hovering over it.

"You can't leave the room."

"Safiya. You're going to—"

Oh shit. The realization of what she's about to do hits me at the same time as a substantial weight slams into me. I'm caught off guard and I topple to the side, driven to the ground with someone sprawled on top of me.

"Zero?" I shout over the roar of the air catching on fire.

She covers my mouth with one hand, my eyes with the other, and ducks her head down to my shoulder. Her skin is rough and wet and that's all I can process before the darkness behind her hand erupts into the whitest light I've ever seen.

The roar of a thousand bombs going off five feet in front of me knocks me senseless.

CHAPTER TWENTY

Aideen

My ears are ringing and the cloth on my back, legs, and arms is on fire, and that's not hyperbole. Coughing and shaking, I roll off Drew and onto the concrete floor, flopping back and forth, snuffing out the flames. Something smells like burning hair. It's my hair, burning. I pat at the ends until they go out, leaving them more ragged than after my attack with the scissors.

"Zero? What the hell?"

I open my mouth to answer but another fit of ragged coughing comes out instead. The air is filled with ash and smoke, and every breath I take burns my lungs.

The ceiling, already the color of chiseled rock, has a patina of lighter ash, fanning out from a tight center point, and that's as clean as things get in Costecu's underground lair. The lightbulb is blown out, but a trickle of light coming from the hallway allows me to see.

The chair and corpse are also gone, roasted into oblivion. No doubt some of the ash is spiraling around in the air, following hidden eddies of current, surfing the dissipating heat waves.

The rest of the ash is Safiya. Was Safiya.

She's dead. She incinerated herself to try to stop Drew. Deep under Costecu's mind manipulation, another dead person on the long list of dead people this conflict has caused. Until a few minutes ago I was right there with her, until the reality of the situation hit me. The threat of Drew ending up dead snapped me out of whatever web Costecu's charm had woven.

In retrospect, it seems stupid. My instinct to cover him with my body was good in principle, but he's so much bulkier than I am, and I'm not sure it did anything. At least it knocked his stupid ass to the floor so he wasn't standing, gaping at his ex-girlfriend like some hungry fish, taking the full force of the blast.

"Zero."

"Huh? I'm fine. What?"

"You're fine?" He drags me to my feet, his hands are on my shoulders before he cups my face, staring into my eyes like he's trying to examine the wrinkles on my brain. It's intimate and confusing in the midst of all the carnage.

"Yes, I'm fine. Really." I shake him off and stomp into the middle of the room, then turn and pace over to one of the other walls, because I don't want to stand in the small circle of ash. That's where Safiya was.

"Are you sure? Because your best friend—"

"Not my best friend," I mumble, searching the corner between the floor and the wall for what?

"Okay. Your work colleague burned herself to cinders, and right before that you were trying to kill me. Maybe I'm wrong, but it doesn't seem like a normal day for you."

"Oh, yeah, sure. And it's normal for you?" I kick at the wall, angry about something. I'm not sure what about yet, but I'll figure it out.

"I mean, kind of. Yeah. I've seen a lot of people die."

"Whoop-dee-doo." I spin around to find him standing right there behind me, looking implacable and steady.

The skin on his face is red where my hands weren't able to protect him from the explosion, the knees of his slacks are dark red from dried blood, and the hems and edges of his clothing is frayed. There are massive rips revealing bruised and cut skin, his beard has blood and ash speckled in it. There's something wrong with the angle of the fingers on his left hand.

He's gorgeous.

"Zero?" He reaches out for me, and before I have an idea what I'm doing, I throw myself into his arms, pressing against his chest and bawling my eyes out.

My outburst lasts all of thirty seconds, while he holds me close without saying anything, and then I peel myself off him and swipe at my wet eyes. The back of my hands hurt. My legs hurt. My jaw hurts. Even with the protective coating of thick skin and the film of weird mucus-water that keeps me from drying out, the flames did a lot of damage to my exposed skin.

"Sorry." I'm not able to look him in the eyes. I'm so weak.

"Hey." He takes my chin in his hand, tilting it up until his gaze catches mine. "There's nothing to be sorry for. There's been a lot of...stuff going on these past few days. It's catching up, and that's fine."

"Yeah, but it's not over." I want to wipe my nose, but I don't want him to stop touching me. I'm reminded of that first moment, when he was secured in the interrogation room. His intense, deep gaze that could melt glass. "Why are you looking at me like that?"

"Like what?"

"Like you want to hit me or something." I shake my head and step out of reach, drained from the outpouring of emotion.

"No, this isn't my want-to-hit-someone face. This is my want-to-fuck-someone face."

I swallow. "Oh. Um. But I'm...I'm..." I gesture at myself. "I'm not particularly attractive with this sealskin going on. Or the burns. Or, um, the blood."

"I like the skin. Reminds me of stone, almost. Like you have carvings on you. Stone tattoos."

"What? That's weird."

"Zero." He steps closer again, forcing me to lift my head. "You think I care what you look like? There are plenty of other beautiful women out there who would be glad to climb this mountain."

"That's kind of egotistical," I mutter.

He holds either side of my face, his hands strong and warm. His eyes bore into me. "I want to fuck you because you're strong, and smart, and you can take care of yourself. You don't need me, and that makes me want you. Badly."

"Oh." It's a good thing he's holding me up, or I might fall over.

He cracks a smile. "Also, I mean, yeah, your tits are fantastic."

"God, I knew it." I slap at his arms and stomp to the other side of the room. "Fucking perv."

"What?" His eyes open in feigned innocence. "I can't like your tits? And you've got a nice caboose, to boot."

I march back over to give him a piece of my mind, but as soon as I'm within arm's reach, he grabs me, tugs me close, and literally dips me back to plant a kiss on my lips. My head spins with the ferocity and strength of it, my hands flail to find purchase, and I no longer care how dry his lips are, how much mine hurt, and that he's rubbing blood-ash from his beard all over my face.

It might as well be the first time he's ever kissed me, with the strength and passion he brings to the connection. I can't think of a more inappropriate place to be making out, but the second his tongue touches the seam between my lips, my jaw drops open.

A brief flash of the future, where we aren't covered in blood and fighting for our lives. We're naked and alone in a natural hot spring with all the time in the world to indulge in every fantasy we've ever had. When he breaks the kiss, I snap back to reality.

"I really like kissing you too," he whispers.

"There's dead people on your face," I whisper back, in an attempt to break the mood. It's feeling serious, and don't I want it to be serious in the middle of Costecu's hideout. I tried to kill him, twice, and I think he broke one of my ribs, and it feels kind of disrespectful to be all lovey-dovey in the same room where Safiya died. And I'm scared. Scared I'll never get the hot spring future.

"It's another Friday," he shrugs. "Are you changing the subject?"

"Um. Yes?"

He chuckles and drags me upright. "I'll let it go this time because we probably ought to find Costecu and stop him. Are you up for it?"

"Just like that?" I try to imagine myself fighting Costecu, and in no way can I find a good outcome. He controlled me as easily as peanut butter controls dogs.

"Yup. Just like that. It's how things work. I decide to do something, and then do it."

"But he's already almost killed you like a million times." He grabs my hand and drags me out of the room of ash. I'll never forget that room, not in my happiest moment or saddest nightmare. His fingers are a bit squishy.

"The key word there is 'almost'. He hasn't, and he won't. He's weaker now, searching for blood. If we can get to him before he fills up, we can do it together."

I'm not sure if his confidence is stupid or correct, but it's sure doing something to me. I keep protesting. "He charmed me so easily."

"Yeah, and then you snapped out of it. Why?"

I look everywhere but at him. "I didn't want to see you hurt," I end up mumbling.

"Sorry, what?" He's grinning, the smug bastard.

"I said, I didn't want to see you hurt," I shout. "Happy?"

"Yup. So, keep feeling that and you're golden."

"Is that what you do?" I intend it to sound snide, but it comes out more like a limp insult.

He drags us to a stop and turns to me. "Yes. If anything happened to you, I'd be sad, devastated beyond belief. I'll never let anything happen to you."

"Except, you know, break my fingers and stuff."

He clenches his jaw, and a flame sparks in his eyes. If he didn't have an iron grip on me, I'd shrink back, because boy he's big and frightening.

"I'm not proud of that, but it had to be done. It was that or let Costecu get you." His face softens, and he frowns. "I'm sorry. I'll make it up to you somehow once we get out of here."

"If we get out of here."

"*Once* we get out of here," he repeats back, his tone brooking no argument or doubt. He starts walking again, his long strides demand I move fast.

"Okay, well, what's the plan, then?"

"Find him, kill him, go home."

I roll my eyes. "Don't you think ahead at all?"

"Thinking gets in the way of actions."

"Dumbass. You think he's going to let you get close? He can probably hear you a mile away. Stop. Hey, stop." I dig in with my heels and while it doesn't stop our forward progress, it slows it down, which is irritating enough he halts and turns around to glare at me.

"Zero, we don't have a lot of time."

"Yeah, so listen to me. He wasn't there when I snapped out of it, right? So let me pretend to still be charmed, and bring you to him like a prisoner or something."

He scoffs. "Okay, sure. Like you could ever subdue me. No offense. An actual six-hundred-pound dragon couldn't put me down."

"You're one stuck-up asshole sometimes, you know that?"

"You like it."

"No, I don't. Shut up and let me think. Let go. I need to pace."

He releases my wrist and leans against the wall of the tunnel, his arms crossed while scanning me up and down.

"Could I say you're knocked out, and back in the room? That Safiya," my voice catches a little. "Took you down? You couldn't be close by if I did that, he'd hear and smell you. I'd have to lead him back to the room."

"I'm not letting you get near him by yourself. No way."

"Well, then come up with something better, and I'm not waiting forever. You're the one who was storming around in a hurry." I roll my hand at him and raise my eyebrows.

"We'll just overpower him and take him out. Two against one. Easy."

"Is that what you do for everything? Seriously? How are you alive?"

"I'm good at it?"

"Yeah? Then why are you still skulking around here? Why haven't you killed him yet? You *do* want to kill him, right?"

He surges off the wall and grabs me on the sides of my head, our glares clashing like thunderclouds. "Don't you dare. Don't you even suggest I don't want to get rid of that scum. I'd gladly die if I knew it would guarantee he would too."

I would be scared if I hadn't been expecting that response: if I hadn't goaded him into it. He's not a complicated a person, which is something I find refreshing. It's nice to know what someone is thinking without having to dig for it. Too many conflicts arise from hidden agendas.

"Then let me help, and you don't have to die." His glare softens but doesn't disappear. "Please. I don't want you to die." I reach up and put my hands over his.

He searches my face for something: truth, determination, I don't know. He must find it because he sighs, blinks, and then nods. "Fuck. Fine. We'll do it your way. But if it doesn't work and he kills you, I'll be super upset."

"You can totally spank me if I don't come back," I whisper.

His eyebrows shoot up. "You'd like that?"

"Maybe. But we'll never find out because you're not going to get the chance," I smirk.

"Liar." He kisses me. It's a different kind of kiss. Not like all the ones before, which were hard, passionate, and dangerous. This one is soft with promises of sweet things to come. He holds it for eternity, until I'm melting into a puddle of selkie goo. When he finally lets my lips go, the soft sound of parting is like a wave hitting the beach, leaving me breathless and a little wet.

"Okay." I swallow the lump in my throat. "I have to come back so I can get more of those, I guess."

It's his turn to smirk and everything is feeling romantic until he grabs my ass and squeezes so hard I yelp.

"Ass."

"Good luck, Zero. See you soon." He spins me toward the throne room and gives me a nudge, then saunters off like he's king of the world.

"You're not that awesome," I shout after him, to which he waves insolently.

I take a big breath, and then five more, not sure if the nerves are from what's happened, what I'm about to do, or both. Probably both.

The path to Costecu's room is well-known. Only about twenty steps down the tunnel and I run into someone, but before I can react in self-defense, they push past me and keep going, too frightened to stop. I'm not going to look a gift horse in the mouth.

I run into people two more times, eliciting the same non-reaction, and when I get to the large entry chamber, I find out why. Bodies are strewn everywhere. It only takes a cursory examination to notice they're all pretty pale and leaking blood out of puncture wounds on their necks. Costecu has been feeding on his own people, which reeks of desperation, and doesn't help me feel any better.

I better get my shit in order. If he hasn't figured out I'm here yet, he will soon, and I need to act charmed. What if he's recovered and charms me permanently? No, no, no. Drew needs me to do this, and more importantly, I need to do it for myself.

This is my responsibility, too. This is the goal I've been working toward for years. I've had the basic training to fortify my mind against charms of all types. I wasn't expecting it the first time Costecu turned it on, but I'll be ready this time. Just because he's a hundreds-of-years old vampire doesn't mean I can't beat him in a mental battle.

I should try to take him into custody. After he's subdued. I should. It's the right thing to do. Deep breath.

Before I get halfway to his door, he calls out.

"Is that a selkie I hear? Dear Aideen, is that you? Do come in, please."

No nerves, no nerves, no nerves.

I step around the bodies and through the ajar door to find Costecu perched back on his chair like everything is fine. I plaster a smile on my face and hope it's not obvious how disgusting he appears. He's smeared with blood, his face, his hands, his arms, his clothes. It smells like iron, and it's disgusting.

"We got him, your highness." That sounds weird. Push forward. "He's not dead but he's close. I thought you might want to be the one to finish him off because you deserve to. Because of how great you are."

That may be overdoing it, but he doesn't seem to notice. Maybe he's so confident it doesn't even enter his mind. That's the bad kind of confidence, the one Drew somehow manages to avoid.

"Ah, yes. How considerate. Indeed, I would like to."

I expect a pressure on my mind, something tugging me to like him. Not that there was last time. It just...happened. This time though, nothing happens. I'm either immune or he's not trying because he thinks I'm still charmed. Or he doesn't care and he's playing with me before he rips my throat out. Yeah, could be that one.

At least I got a good kiss out of Drew first.

"Your heart rate is increasing, dear. Is everything okay?"

"Oh, yup. Excited to see you kill Lindberg. He's so vile and nasty. Not like you at all, you sexy beast."

"Then let us go. Will you be my escort?"

"I'd be delighted." Suppressing the shudder as he holds out his elbow for me to loop my arm through, we make our way back to the torture room. His arm is so thin and bony, and if I hadn't seen what he could do, I wouldn't believe there's any way this frail vampire could cause so much damage. I might be able to snap him in half. Except that's not true. I'd be dead before I tried.

Why was this a good idea, again? How the hell are we going to take him out?

Two against one, that's what Drew said. But Costecu killed fifteen of his own people in short order with no effort.

This is a bad idea.

We're going to die.

CHAPTER TWENTY-ONE

Druian

As soon as Zero is around the corner where she can't see my reaction, I slump against the wall and cover my face in my hands. This is a bad idea. She's going to get herself killed and it's going to be all my fault. I turn to go get her, take two steps, then spin around and take two steps the other way. I need to trust her. I need to let her do this. She can do it, she's smart, tough, all those things. I shouldn't baby her.

The need to protect her is strong. I need to be there in case something goes wrong. This time it's five steps before I whirl around and go back. If I'm there, I'll only put her in danger. I can't walk into the room with her. Costecu would snap her neck right away.

She can do it. I have to trust her. She can do it.

I go back and forth along the corridor for at least three minutes, fighting between going to help and letting her do it herself. It goes against everything I believe to leave her to the wolves, but I've got to learn to relax.

The march back to the torture room is, well, torture, but I make myself do it. Once there, there's nothing to do but wait, and stare at the patterns of ash and scorch marks on the rock walls. I touch one of the streaks, as if I'll feel something new or more about Safi: discover a hidden well of emotion, a connection beyond physical attraction we never quite had. I don't. There's nothing but residual sadness at the passing of another person.

Not to be callous, but Zero is my person. I feel more about her skinning her knee than another death in all my journeys.

"Sorry you went out that way, Safi," I mutter to myself. It doesn't feel like enough, but nothing ever does. There's nothing you can say to a friend who's died, because they can't hear your pretty words. It does no good talking to yourself either. You already know what you're feeling. The only thing to do is try to make sure it doesn't happen to anyone else, and not feel guilty when it does anyway, despite all your hard work.

I better figure out what I'm going to do. I can't attack Costecu head on. He's going to be stupid strong, and I'll have to use some tools besides my fists if I want to get out of this alive. At the very least, Zero's got to get out alive. I hope all this subterfuge is worth it, because it makes me itchy. I'd rather punch things.

Casting about the room, I search it and my brain for any ideas. I hate trying to figure out things like this. It's like trying to solve a puzzle without all the pieces. How am I supposed to know what to do when I can't control everything?

Okay, so what weakens vampires? Beheading does it. Puncturing the heart. There's no wood bigger than a splinter left after that inferno. That'd kill him outright, too. I guess if I had ten pounds of garlic I could shove it down his throat. He'd get a runny nose from that, and maybe he'd choke on it all. Drown him in water. Shoot him with a silver bullet. All of those things work on pretty much anyone. They're nothing special to vamps. Unfortunately, I don't have a river or a gun tucked into my pockets.

I scratch my beard and watch some ash float to the floor. I'm sure as fuck going to need a bath after this. A real long one. With Zero. We won't get out of for several hours. I want to see that healing power of hers up close and personal, and then everything else up close and personal.

Wait. I scratch again. More ash. Hold on. Isn't dried up blood supposed to hurt vampires? Something about them needing live blood, so if you give them "dead" blood it wrecks their circulatory system. Or something like that anyway. I've never had to care about memorizing every part of vampiric lore since I've never met one I couldn't behead before.

This ash is Safi, and whoever that other person was. Some chair, too, but a lot of people. Two people. It's got to have dead blood in it. It has everything: skin, hair, organs, all the things inside people. If dead blood hurts vamps, imagine what dead liver does.

I start scooping as much as I can into a pile on the floor with my hands, which is something I've never done before. Gathering up someone's ash. I've kicked ash around after burning corpses and people, but I never stopped to ponder it. Dead people, reduced to a greyish-white powder. Weird. It's so simple. I'd kind of prefer to be buried under a massive headstone, myself. One that I'll carve with my own hands, that'll last for centuries.

I'll think about that later. Right now, it's time to contemplate how satisfying it's going to be to snuff Costecu for once and all with this handful of ash. I'm going to jam it in his mouth and watch him wither away into more ash while I flip him the bird. With both hands.

Zero's words burn in my skull. Why didn't I kill him before? Because I couldn't. Because he's strong. Because I'm worried if I take him out, someone else will rise up to take his place. That's why I stayed here, sabotaging as much as I could, slowing him down, keeping his successes as minimal as possible.

Yes, some people had to be thrown into the flames, but that's life. Not everyone can be a winner, and if I hadn't taken them out, someone else probably would have. A lot slower, too. Some of the creeps around here are quite the sadists.

Not like most of the people I took out were innocent. Far from it. Killers, psychos, misanthropes. You can't tell me the world's not a better place because I killed them before they could do more damage. There's enough horrible shit people have to worry about, and a ghoul eating them shouldn't be one of them.

Unwanted memories of corpses dance in front of me in the empty room. Prominent are the faces of Safi and poor person strapped to the chair I strangled less than an hour ago. The one I choked to death while fighting the banshee. I could've stopped myself from strangling him, except it would've tipped off Costecu I wasn't under his control. He would've disposed of me right then and there, and then Zero would have walked in here without any way for me to protect her. Costecu would have killed her and Safi.

I killed a stranger to save Zero. I'll have to live with it, as I've lived with everything I've done to get to this point. To end Costecu, and to save Zero.

I take a breath and loosen my fists, bending down to scoop up some of the ash that filtered out when I squeezed my fingers too tight. My knuckles are scraped and cracked from fighting. My fingers ache from being broken. They're not quite knitted back together yet. Soon I won't have to fight anyone anymore. I'll be dead, but Costecu will be dead, and Zero will be alive, and that's what matters. She can be happy her job is done and the world is a better place.

The waiting is killing me. Costecu might be killing me in a minute. I laugh at the morbidity of my situation. I wonder what's taking so long. There might be a problem, something I need to help Zero with. But no, I need to stay here. Let her do her job, she can do it. She's alone with a monster. She'll be here any time now.

When this is over, what's she going to do? Probably therapy for a while, and hopefully a vacation. She needs a long vacation. Somewhere she doesn't need to come back from. In fact, she should probably move, get out of here. Maybe I can convince her to leave with my dying breath and do something less dangerous than stalking vampires.

Yeah, I'm going to die here. It doesn't bother me because it's what I've wanted since the start. Once Costecu is dead I won't need to do anything else, and I'd rather not be stuck with all my terrible memories. I'd like them to go away. I'm tired of them bouncing around my head every night when I try to sleep.

Except for all the lurid dreams I have about Zero. Not that I've slept a whole lot since I kidnapped her, but I kind of want to dream about her. I can't stop thinking about her. Would Safi have volunteered to go into the lion's den and drag the monster out? No disrespect to the dead, but no. She was fun, but that's all anyone I've ever been with was: fun. Zero isn't fun. She's serious.

I have to gather up the ash for the third time because my hands have gone slack. They'll be here soon, for sure. Pay attention. Get this right, and everything's done. I can't let her down.

There's no more room for worries or fears or hopes or dreams. All that can come later. If there is a later. There's only room for doing my job. Everything else can wait.

Taking up position next to the doorway, out of sight of the window, I take deep breaths to slow my heartbeat. Deeper to push my metabolism to slower than if I were asleep. It's a neat dwarven trick, and it comes in handy when trapped in a rockfall underground. Costecu will believe I'm passed out.

Thoughts slow. Everything is slow. Footsteps. Voices.

"Is your friend guarding his body, dear girl? I don't hear her heartbeat."

"She died putting him down," Zero says, calm as anything. She sounds like a professional. She sounds like me.

"Ah. What a sweet gesture."

In slow motion they walk into the room next to me. She's got her arm in his. He's hunched and small and bloody and it's all a show. A lie, a falsehood, and this is fucking *it*.

Everything stretches out as I wake myself up, like in those movies when things go to lightspeed, and then in a snap of light and sound I'm knocking Zero aside, plowing into Costecu, and slamming my hands over his mouth and eyes with the loudest roar I can manage.

He's quick to react, almost too quick, and half the stuff ends up smeared on his face as we tumble to the ground.

"Run Zero," I shout, because she needs to get far away from here.

"Kill him," Costecu screams at the same time, and the wave of charm frays the wrinkles of my brain. I've only got a split second to wonder if it worked on her before she lands on top of me with a thump.

I wait for the teeth in my neck while still trying to rub as much ash into Costecu's mouth as I can, not sure if it's doing anything, and he's starting to get up. Zero isn't attacking me, though, she's helping. She's wrapped around his legs and holding on tight.

"Go," I shout again, desperate. She's got to get out of here.

"Not a fucking chance," she growls back, her eyes narrowed in a way I'm starting to learn is her being stubborn. There's not a trace of doubt or charm in her eyes. Whatever he's trying to do clearly isn't working.

Costecu manages to get up, throwing her off his legs in a surge. I cling on tight around his neck, draped over his back like a seven foot, three-hundred-pound backpack.

He's going to have to rip off my arms to get me to let go.

The gritty feeling of the ash as it smears against my palm is not something I want to dwell on, so it's lucky I'm too busy concentrating on keeping my footing, his face away from me, and squeezing until something breaks.

He gets an arm free when I shift my grip to more of a bear hug, distracting me until too late to warn Zero not to do what she does. A crazed look flashes in her eyes, the pupils blown out to blackness. It's an uncomfortable reminder seals are not vegetarians, and selkies are not cuddly. I've got one second to plant a foot behind me before she leaps on us, right in Costecu's face, teeth bared and snapping.

The worst place to attack a vampire is near the mouth, which is obvious to anyone in their right mind, but it's hard to stop instinct without a lot of practice and some luck.

I manage to keep his arm contained, although he's straining to move it down and grab her, but there's nothing I can do about his teeth. The angle I'm at gives me the perfect view of them puncturing her skin in the side of her neck.

"Zero, no," I shout as my heart pounds in my ears. Frantic to get them apart, I lose all sense of self-preservation, letting go of Costecu to grab at them in an attempt to pull him off of her. It's a small consolation she's got her teeth around his neck, too. Last I checked, selkies don't drain their victims of blood in a matter of minutes.

Neither one is willing to let go as I grab at their faces, arms, and bodies, dragging them to the ground as they cling tight in some macabre embrace, the sound of flesh being broken and blood flowing slithering under my incoherent shouts. Every moment he's attached to her she's closer to death, her life-force being sucked out of her.

"Zero. Damn it, let go," I roar, frantic as I've ever been.

Nothing I shout does any good. Damned stubborn, she glares at me, her jaw locked around his jugular like a dog holding on to a Christmas ham.

Anger and desperation give me strength, and I haul them upright by the back of Zero's body armor, spin, and slam Costecu into the wall, again and again.

"Let her go, you bastard, let her go. I'll fucking kill you a fucking thousand times if you kill her. Let her go."

He ignores me, and if the battering I'm giving him is affecting him at all, he doesn't show it. I slam and bash, and when that doesn't work, I toss them down again and grab his jaw with my hands, trying to slip a finger into his mouth to pry it open. I don't care if I lose it, maybe if he tastes my blood, he'll give up on her. Anything.

It could be hours, but is probably only seconds. With a spasm, then a shudder, Zero slackens. I pull her off and away, although I have to kick Costecu in the head several times to get his mouth loose. They're both dazed and bloody, hideous red and swollen marks on their necks, bleeding oceans of red.

I pull Zero up, leaning her against me as I crouch on the ground, attempting to stop the flow of blood with my hand. When that doesn't work, I yank at a rip in my shirt, tearing fabric in a jagged angle until I get a piece to hold against her wound.

Costecu burbles a laugh, clamping a hand to the wound she left on his neck and scoots on his butt to the other side of the room. "I think, ah-ha-ha, I think that was an ill-advised attack. Is this your plan, Mr. Lindberg? To have your attack dog maul me? I believe it's failed."

I ignore him, although my blood is boiling in fury. "Zero. Hey. Zero. Why'd you have to go and do that?"

She coughs. "To protect you."

"No, Zero, no." The words get stuck in my throat like boulders. I have to force them out. "I'm supposed to protect you."

"Misogynist. I can take—" she coughs again, specks of blood spattering my sleeve. "Care of myself."

"You're not doing a great job of it right now." I tear another swath from my shirt and wad it against the wound. Her flinch as I press it against her breaks my heart.

"I'm fine." She pushes at my arms, weaker than any push before. Her hands are like the caress of a soft breeze. "You ought to...finish it. Not going to let me...get the glory, are you?"

Costecu picks that moment to cackle again. "What a touching scene. The two lovers, twisted in their own fates. The final moments before their world is shattered to pieces. It would make a fantastic tragic romance."

"I'll be right back," I whisper to Zero, taking her hand and pressing it against the cloth before propping her in the corner of the room. "Don't go anywhere."

"Wouldn't...dream of it."

I rip off the rest of my shirt, wad it up, and stuff it behind her head as the worst pillow in history.

Turning around before she can see my face and the wrath I'm sure is etched on it, I advance on Costecu. He pulls himself to his feet and tilts his head up in challenge.

He's too slow to react, as I grab him by the collar and slam my fist into his face. His jaw is hard, like a diamond, and whether it's my fist or his teeth breaking, I don't know or care. He grabs at me as I hit him again and again, until someone's fresh blood is smearing across his face, mixing in with the darker red of dried blood and ash.

He's laughing or maybe talking, or trying to talk, but nothing he can say or do matters. He's also not resisting, but I'm too angry to care to figure out why. Nothing matters but plastering his brains against my fist.

Then in one moment, with a crack that shakes down my arm, his jaw flies off, a twisted bird of bone, smashing into the wall and shattering. His eyes widen and there's finally fear there. Stunned, I pause in my assault.

Zero's shaky voice draws both of our attention. "Ever heard of seal finger? You've...got selkie finger. Bacteria. It's fast, and way worse. I imagine your joints are pretty...much frozen..." She trails off into more coughing.

Costecu has a dazed look on his face, his tongue flopping around in the air. He tries to say something, but it comes out as gurgles.

I rear back my fist one last time. I'd planned for this moment, but I never knew what I would say. What witty quip would I come up with? Nothing ever seemed appropriate or good enough. In this moment, nothing would ever be good enough.

Words don't matter. Actions do.

My fist meets his forehead with a crack, the back of his head smacks into the wall, and his skull comes apart like a watermelon under a sledgehammer. I let his body crumple to the floor, leaning against the wall and glaring down at the headless mess who was the terror of my past life.

"Can we go now?" Zero mumbles.

I run over and catch her as she slides down the wall to the floor, my future life.

As long as I can save her.

CHAPTER TWENTY-TWO

Aideen

Costecu's head exploding between Drew's fist and the wall is a sight I'll never forget. It's haunting, and not a thing I'd want to see ever again, but a small part of me rejoices. It's over. He's stopped. Drew is okay. I've done what I need to do. Everything goes black.

There's a brief moment of searing brightness where I might be drowning, or might be on fire, or might be having a great orgasm, but it's all muddled and confused and I'm in no state to process or understand.

Sounds and smells reach through whatever veil I'm under. Blood and death, shouting, feet pounding on the floor, someone punching a button a million times, all the clicks running together into a machine gun of irritation.

"Stop it," I moan, then pass out again.

Heavy breathing on my face, cool air against my skin, doors slamming, an engine.

"Stay with me, Zero, stay with me," someone says. Drew? I slump against the window.

"Not goin' anywhere," I say. My face is wet. Sweat, tears, blood, who knows.

Colors flash behind my eyes, even though they're closed, unless they're flashing in front of my eyes. I don't want to open them to find out. It'll only get brighter. Everything is bright and sharp and achy, and some asshole keeps moaning. It might be me.

Something hurts, and it might be everything, but it's too nebulous and all-consuming to know where from. Everything is wrong.

"Wzzt?" I ask, not sure what I'm asking, or who I'm asking it to, or what answer I want to get. My tongue feels like a brick.

"We're almost there, Zero. Hang in there. No quitting, you hear me?"

"I dun quit."

"There's the Zero I know."

A hand pats my thigh and it hurts like a billion needles. "Ow, ow, ow."

"Sorry."

After an interminable number of minutes, I figure out I'm in a car and Drew's probably driving because it sounds like his voice. The car stops, my door opens, and I would've flopped to the ground, but someone catches me. Everything is so bright.

"Lindberg?"

"Yup. I've got you."

"I can walk," I protest through swollen lips and a sore throat.

"No, you can't."

"Yes." I make no attempt to move.

The sound of traffic I hadn't recognized goes away, fading into silence. Except for someone saying something. Why do they have to be so loud? Drew's voice rumbles something back to whoever, and I try to move closer to his chest to feel it. It's a nice rumble. Maybe he'll say something else.

"A couple more minutes," he says, but not as rumbly.

I huff. "Rumble."

"What?"

I crack open an eye, although it hurts like hell. "Condo?"

"Yes, we're at your condo."

"Why?" I regret asking because something in my neck pops and Lindberg curses.

"I'll buy you a new door," he says, which makes no sense. There's nothing wrong with my door.

My neck is warm, my toes feel cold, and there's some crazy shattering, splintering explosion around us. I'd like to scream in terror because it feels like the right thing to do, but nothing happens when I open my mouth. Oh well. I'll try later.

Everything is all jiggly and shaky. Maybe we're having an earthquake. That would be odd. Something slams, and then I go down, away from Lindberg. I clutch at him because he's nice and warm and I'm freezing cold, but he peels my hands away.

"It's okay," he says.

It's not okay. He's gone. Is he going to come back?

A rushing noise drowns out my thoughts, and ice-cold liquid hits my feet. I can't move to get away from it as it creeps up to my calves, but by the time it's at my knees it's lukewarm, and then within a few seconds it's warm, then hot.

Hot water, amazing hot water, lapping at my legs and hips, climbing higher by the moment. It's so comforting, except my clothes are still on. I can't take a bath dressed. That's ridiculous.

I attempt speech, working my jaw open and closed, trying to remember how to use muscles and breath to form words, but nothing responds, and everything feels strange. I manage a huff of breath that turns to a whistle.

"Don't talk, Zero. Relax. I'm going to get your clothes off."

That's good. I wouldn't want them to get ruined in the water, and now I can get warmer. Need to be really warm, because my toes and fingers are still cold, even though they're soaking in hot bathwater.

He pulls me forward so my back isn't resting against the side of the tub and tugs at the bottom of my shirt. It's already wet and heavy, the rushing water at my waist. I want the jets on, but have no way to communicate that. The remains of my black top comes up and off, catching on my chin for a second, and the unwelcome cold air batters against me.

"Almost there," he says right by my ear. His bulk is leaning over me, one hand on my back while the other unhooks my bra with one easy twist. If I wasn't so cold and sleepy, that move would've been impressive.

Uncontrollable shakes overtake me as I'm lowered down into the tub. The water isn't high enough yet, coming up only to below my breasts.

"Damn it, why is your tub so big? It's taking forever to fill."

The jets would help with that. I don't know how to tell him without moving or speaking, neither of which is an option. I try telepathy, but he must not notice.

Through my blurry vision that won't clear, I watch him reach under the water and then he's fumbling with my pants in that slow motion way that happens underwater. His fingers dig into my thighs a little too hard, and the soaking fabric sticks to my wounds, making the process difficult. He grumbles, which is almost a rumble, as he fights with my clothing.

"Zero, these were hot as hell, but they're pissing me off."

I'd laugh if I could. Drew, defeated by pants. Bet that's never happened before. He gets them past my thighs, and then it goes easier. The heavy slapping sound they make as they hit the tile floor of my bathroom is like a gunshot.

"You're still shaking."

The water is up to my shoulders, and although I can tell it's hot, the cold is spreading.

"Fuck, work. Come on," he demands.

I slip down the side of the tub as the water rises to my neck and the friction goes away. Lindberg catches me under an arm and turns off the faucet. Then he's stepping into the water, nudging me forward, and sliding down behind me like the comfiest rock on earth. One of his arms wraps around my waist and holds me secure against him, the other pushes wet tips of hair from between us and over my shoulder.

"Take a breath, Zero. We're going under."

Not sure I could take that breath, but he won't let me drown. Plus, I doubt we'll be under for longer than the ten minutes I can hold my breath. I surrender to the water underworld. My blurry vision gets blurrier, and most sound drops away replaced by the insulating properties of water. It's peaceful and warm, and I want to go to sleep and rest for a long time.

Maybe I do sleep. I'm floating in heaven, but then the buzzing sneaks up on me and overtakes everything. A thousand miniature needles hammer my skin all over every inch, and it's horrible and painful and I want it to go away. The only resistance I can manage is weak swipes of my hands over whatever skin is close. Bubbles pour from my mouth as I attempt a breath like an idiot.

In an instant we surface, Drew pulls my head above water, where I spit and sputter out the water invading my throat, searing down into my lungs and stomach.

"I've got you Zero, you're okay. You're fine. Calm down, it's okay."

I cough, spitting up pink fluid. "Hrrng." I push at his arm, then clap a hand to my neck where the buzzing has increased to a throbbing hammer. Where it was cold, now it's burning hot, like a fire poker being pressed against my neck.

"Can you talk? Tell me what's going on."

"Hurts, argh," I gasp through a rough throat and burning lungs. Pain shoots up my left side, causing my toes to curl in a spasm.

"Where?"

It takes a ragged couple of inhales before I have the air to answer. "Everything. Ass."

He laughs.

"'S not funny."

"No, it's not. I'm laughing because you're going to be okay."

"Course I am." I pause to ride out a thrilling crackle of electricity through my hands and wrists. "I'm fine."

"Zero, you weren't fine. I'm guessing half of your bones were broken, you had burns all over your skin, I have no idea what internal injuries you sustained, and the artery in your neck Costecu weakened popped as soon I got here, spraying blood like a hose all over your nice things. Now you're resting in water that's red and black from blood and dirt, and you're still trying to fight me."

That's a lot to take in, but the worst part is the dirty water, maybe because it's easier to process. "You know, tubs have drains. You can empty the...the...oh, fuck..." The buzzing from my body repairing and regenerating has traveled from my arms and legs inward, concentrating in my chest and stomach.

I've never had to go through a repair process this intense. Broken fingers, toe stuff, the accidental gash or minor cut. A sprain once, from stumbling over a rock when jogging. Each time the buzzing had been annoying but minor, and not long-lasting.

This time it's a hundred times more painful. I hadn't been paying attention, shoving the sensations away as per normal, but it's invaded my insides, unavoidable. I didn't think a liver or stomach could tingle, but they're doing their best.

"Zero, what's wrong?"

"Ah...the repairing...I've never felt it in my...organs. Hnrg." I grip his arm tight and don't care if it's hurting, because he's a big boy and he can handle it. This sensation is so weird. I duck my chin down to my chest, squeeze my eyes shut, and attempt to ride it out.

To my horror, the tingles morph into *those* types of tingles and sweep down into my core, the last spot I want them to go, but the last place left untouched by the regeneration.

"No, no, no, no, no..." I mumble, then bite my lip and hold onto his arm harder.

"Zero? Uh..."

I try to hold it in, to dampen it down, but there's no stopping the shakes in my legs and trembles in my stomach as the merciless tingles explode inside and then pour out of me in a rush of sensation and pleasant warmth.

There's a second or two of utter silence as I try to catch my breath.

"I'm flattered. I had no idea my presence was that awe-inspiring."

"Shut up," I mumble, and then my face heats in embarrassment as a wave of vulnerability rolls over me. The moment was so private, so intimate. It was something not in my control, and he was here to see it in all its glory, every unplanned second.

He takes my chin, gentler than I would've expected, and turns my face. I don't open my eyes as they start to burn in the corners.

"Are you...?"

I don't answer, and he doesn't follow up with any more questions. A few seconds of silence tug at my worries, and all the things he might say to make fun of me run laps around my imagination. Then I'm tipping forward, for a moment afraid he's going to dunk me, but instead I hear a pop and a glug and the water starts draining out of the tub. He pulls me back against his chest and his wet shirt.

"What are you doing?" I whisper, wanting to curl into a ball.

"Draining the dirty water of course. Can't have you lounging in this now that you seem to be on the mend. How do you feel?"

Is he really not going to tease me or poke me, or make any more self-satisfied remarks? I'm a little disappointed. "Uh. Fine. I guess."

"Excellent."

The water creeps down the sides of the tub, leaving me exposed. I squeeze my eyes closed tighter, as if that will help to protect me, and fight the shivers.

He shifts me again, drawing back, pulling me away from him, which is the last and first place I want to be. A couple of quiet grunts accompany a rocking back and forth. He shifts the arms holding me, a wet slap echoes across the tiles, two strong hands grip around my waist, turn me around and pull me down against warm and damp skin.

"What are you doing?"

"You're shivering. I'm keeping you warm until everything drains and I can fill it with warm water again."

"Oh." My brain has shut down. I'm sleepy from the regeneration and the unexpected orgasm. Warm tendrils fight with cold icicles running up and down my back and into my stomach.

For some reason my hands are resting on his chest. "There's a button for jets," I say before he can deduce my salacious thoughts. It's freeing for someone to be worried about my well-being, more than in a platonic friend sort of way. He could have dumped me in the tub and then left, or called emergency services, or any of a hundred other non-personal things. Instead, he got into the tub with me, clothes and all, and he's not even making any lewd comments.

"I saw buttons, but I didn't want to push anything in case it might hurt you."

"What's going to hurt me in a tub?"

"Well, aren't you full of vinegar," he chuckles, his hands caressing up and down my back, spreading warmth. "I don't know how strong those jets are. I didn't want water smashing into you, especially if you had internal injuries."

I could tell him it wouldn't matter at, since I was in the water and would've healed, but I don't want to burst his bubble. That he was worried is sweet.

It's a strange type of sweet, but it's what he is, and what he's been the whole time. He tries to hide it with a bossy exterior and physical intimidation, not to mention his large size and fierce visage, but he can't hide it from me anymore. I know it's there.

"I'm going to fall asleep," I mumble, fighting my heavy lids as the last of the water trickles over my toes.

"Let me put you to bed."

"Don't have one."

"What? You don't have a bed?" His beard is scratchy and tickly against my ear.

"Did. Had to throw it out. Tell you later."

"Okay. Couch?"

"Fill tub. Stay here."

He shifts, the muscles in his chest moving against my fingers, and then the water comes on again.

"Hot. Jets."

"Yes ma'am," he chuckles.

The sound of water realigning echoes through the room, and then all the jets come on, spraying the hot water as the tub starts to fill again. It's as close to being under a waterfall as I could manage to buy.

"Take off pants," I say before I regret it.

The noise he makes is less of a chuckle and more of the rumble I wanted before. I'm jostled around a bit, shifted from left to right as he pulls on things. I keep my eyes shut and slide a hand up to hold the back of his head.

Everything settles back down, and there's no longer the cold pinch of a belt buckle or the drag of cloth pants. It's only Drew and me. The way it should be.

"Better?" he asks.

"Mmm."

He says my name, but I'm already slipping into dreams.

CHAPTER TWENTY-THREE

Druain

"Zero? Zero?" I have a moment of panic as her eyes flutter closed, but her breathing slows, not stops, and then she lets loose the most satisfying sigh I've ever heard. She isn't dying: she's fallen asleep. In the tub, filled with hot water, jets pounding away, and the only thing keeping her from drowning is my arms. I couldn't be happier.

After I while my muscles start to get stiff, although whether that's from not moving an inch so I don't disturb her, or from the battering I've taken over the past couple of days, I couldn't say. She might have the ability to rapidly heal in water, but for me it'll take time. My legs start twitching, angry at being kept still. I'll have to move.

An inch at a time, I sit up, cradling her against my chest, careful not to make any sudden movements. My back is not happy at needing to support us in the transition from leaning to sitting forward, but that's too bad.

It's harder to stand. Not that she's heavy, but the inch-by-inch movement strains my leg muscles, already past the point of comfort, and my knees are still not healed all the way. I'll be damned if I let them tell me what to do. My body isn't a temple, it's a machine designed to do my bidding.

A careful step up and over the edge of the tub, a scary moment where my one leg holding us both upright wants to start cramping, and then I'm out of the tub. Zero is still sleeping in my arms like the sexiest baby ever. That's a weird thought. She's no baby, that's for sure.

Padding over to the tall linen closet built into the wall, I balance her in my arms while grabbing at a towel, accidentally knocking a pile to the floor in the process. It's a weird juggling act, but I manage to kind of dry her off, and pat some of the water out of her hair so I'm not exposing her wet body to air. The last thing she needs is to get a cold after all of this. Imagining Zero to have beaten everything, only to be stuck in bed with the sniffles is funny, but also not happening on my watch.

I tuck the towel around her as well as I can. The wet footprints are a reminder of my gentle intrusion into her life. A peek into her bedroom finds she doesn't have a bed. The floor is remarkably clean and shiny, and the space where the bed was is obvious, but it's not there. That's a puzzle for a later date.

Moving into the living area, tossing a quick glance at her shattered front door to make sure no one's hanging around outside, I lower her to one of her couches, pulling a pillow to the armrest for her to lie on. The tiny sound of dissatisfaction she makes as I let her go causes my heart to beat faster.

"I'll be right back, Zero," I whisper in her ear, giving it a quick kiss and pushing damp tendrils of hair away from her face.

Blankets first, then the door. A trip into the bedroom and a shuffle through the closet yields a thin sheet and a thick duvet. I take both. I put the duvet on first, then pause, take it off, and drape the sheet over her first, then the duvet. That way if she gets hot, she can take off the thickest one. I've never had to consider the ramifications of covers. I tend to toss and turn so much by the time I'm awake, everything is bunched up on the floor. Dwarves don't get cold.

Satisfied she's as comfortable as possible, I head to her front door I'd kicked down earlier in my determination to get her to water. There's not too much I can do to fix it, not without several tools, or a new door, but I manage to wrestle it into a propped-up position so it doesn't fall over, and people can't peek inside. For extra security I pick up an end table from the living room and wedge it against the door. Anyone trying to get in will make noise and I'll notice.

No one's going to get within fifty feet of Zero without my say so, not until I can figure out who's safe and who isn't. Costecu had moles, and might have more than I'm aware, and even though he's dead and can't charm anyone, I'm not taking any chances.

No one will hurt her again.

I take a quick detour to poke around in her closet, searching for something I might be able to wear, but give up thirty seconds in.

There's no way she'll have anything that'll fit me, and it's not much of a big deal if I need to walk around naked.

Checking on her once again, finding her still safely asleep, I clean up the wet clothes in the bathroom, wash out the blood and dirt in the tub as best as I can, and dry surfaces with a dark green towel pulled from the fallen pile I'd left on the floor. Not seeing anywhere to put dirty clothes, I drape them over the edge of the tub to dry.

Resisting the urge to stop and thumb her cheek as I move past into the kitchen, I raid the fridge for something to eat and drink. There's not a lot. One bottle of beer and a couple yogurt cups would not be a satisfying snack, but nothing else is unexpired.

I take the bottle with me, set it on the coffee table, and pick up her feet to settle myself down on the other end of the couch, dropping them back in my lap. She's had a whole lot of stuff happen to her, and although I want to wrap her up like a swaddled baby, I don't know what's going to happen when she wakes up. People deal with dangerous and traumatic situations in different ways, and the last thing I want to do is frighten her.

With any luck, once she's awake, she'll be the feisty and stubborn Zero who caught my attention. Then we can talk, along with other things.

Exhaustion sweeps over me. It's all over. Costecu is dead. For real dead. Costecu is dead and I'm alive, somehow, against all odds and wishes. So many memories I don't want to have anymore. Memories I was planning to get rid of by dying. Maybe I can replace them with nice memories instead. Crowd my brain with happiness until all the horror is squeezed out.

I've been stroking Zero's bare ankle this whole time, as it peeks out from under the duvet. It's a nice ankle on a nice foot, attached to a nice leg, part of a damn fine woman.

I'd kind of like to get to know her more than stubborn Zero and naked Zero. For all I know, in her free time she's a hard-drinking, motorcycle-riding, nymphomaniac.

If she is, she disguises it well. Right now, asleep, tucked against the back corner of the couch, the top of her head barely poking out from under the blankets, she could be the sweetest person ever. I wouldn't've been able to guess she could turn into a vicious biting machine at a moment's notice or imagine the tenacity with which she gets a target and doesn't let go. Two years chasing Costecu without a break.

My body wants to fall asleep, but I can't. It's not safe for Zero, and I won't rest on the job. The local cell will crumble without Costecu and his planning, but it'll take some time. Not everyone is going to abandon the cause. They could come here and try to kill Zero, and there could be people in her organization who want her dead.

I study the hallway to stay awake, down where the broken door is, and content myself with rubbing her foot. The arch is soft and still slightly wrinkled from the bath, and the ball is not calloused like mine. The whole thing is smooth. Of course, it would be, with the way she regenerates in water. It's like stroking a rose, one I'm desperate not to crush. I let go and set her foot down. The last thing she needs to wake up to is a broken foot because I'm so hungry to touch her I can't control myself.

I rub my open palm up and down her shin, something that won't lead to crushing or bruising or anything else. It's smooth, too. Does she shave? She must, right? Eternal youth doesn't mean no body hair. She's got *some*. I mean, I wasn't that far out of it at the cabin. That image will be seared into my mind forever. It was too sculpted to be random. She must shave her legs, and all the other stuff. I'll ask her when she wakes up, because that's not a weird question to put out there in our current situation.

I'm not too delirious to realize I'm delirious with lack of sleep and a complete lack of adrenaline. I shouldn't have a problem staying awake, I've stayed awake for days on end before. Those situations were a lot more dire, but this situation could be more dire than I realize. I have no idea one way or another.

Slapping myself in the face, welcoming the sting and the heat to fight back the insidious sluggishness threatening my wakefulness, I pull my hand off of her leg. The temptation to go higher is strong, but it would be super inappropriate while she's sleeping. Being awake would be one thing, when she could growl and slap my hand away. That would be fun. It's not fun if she has no choice.

My thoughts spiral along all sorts of paths, from the ways I want to show Zero how much I care for her, to the ways I want to show Zero how much I want her. Two extremes of the same desire to be around her all the time. I also wonder what kind of take-out she likes best, why she sculpts her pubes, how many hours a day she's actually in her condo, and if she has any friends.

The meandering roads of questions keep me occupied while I make up answers and then ask more questions. I want to know the smallest detail about her, and if I have my way, I will. It might take days, weeks, months, or years, but what choice do I have? Not knowing about her isn't an option.

I lose track of time, with not so much as an old clock ticking nearby to mark the seconds, and my phone lost somewhere in the chaos, the only indication I have that time passes is the daylight fading to dusk, and then deepening to night, casting the room into darkness. A single bar of artificial white light from the hallway outside the apartment breaks through the gap between her ruined door and the frame, throwing jagged patterns on the floor.

"Mgphmn," Zero mumbles and turns in her sleep, bringing my attention to her.

I wait.

"Fnng. Hnmm? Mmm. What...huh? What?" She cycles through the waking moments, and then her hand appears over the edge of the duvet and her eyes peek over the top at me. With my excellent night vision, I can see the expression on her face, one of uncertainty, confusion, and questions.

"It's me, Zero," I whisper as I feel her body tense.

Her muscles relax, and then tense up again. "Drew?"

"Yup."

"You're in my condo."

"Yup."

Her eyes flicker around the room as they adjust to the darkness. "I'm not dead?"

"Not yet."

Her feet withdraw from my lap, and she sits up a tiny bit clutching the duvet to her. "I'm naked. You're naked."

That hadn't even crossed my mind, but I am. "You didn't have any dresses my size."

Her eyebrows lower and she doesn't laugh, but I'm starting to get the hang of her expressions. She doesn't laugh because she feels it wouldn't be appropriate to laugh, but I'd bet inside she's grinning.

"Lights on," she announces, and for a second I think she's commanding me. I'm halfway through a fantasy of how I'd correct that before all the lights in the condo blaze into being.

"Ow, ow. Warn a guy," I protest, covering my eyes against the sudden blindness.

"I did say 'lights on,'" she huffs. "What happened?"

Down to business. I can appreciate that. She likely needs to ground herself, figure out what the current situation is to feel comfortable. The unknown is not her ally.

"Let's see," I start, ticking off things on my fingers. "You broke into Costecu's hideout, helped me take him down, permanently, by wrestling with him and poisoning him, remind me not to let you bite me, and then I got you back to your condo where I saved your life because your jugular burst, and then I washed you, and then you fell asleep for about eight hours."

She stares at me with a face so blank I could write a math problem on it. "What time is it?"

"Don't know. You don't seem to have any clocks here, and I have no idea where our phones are. It's dark outside. You know, you could say 'thank you,'" I add, raising my eyebrows and leaning sideways in her direction.

"For what?"

"The whole...jugular, saving your life thing."

Her arms come out of the duvet to cross over her chest. Her bare shoulders are smooth and perfect, demanding to be grabbed and bitten. "You got me in that mess to start with. If you wouldn't have gone and gotten yourself captured at the cabin—"

"I'm sorry, what? That was *my* fault?" Is she for real? My blood pressure starts to rise, and I grab the thick duvet in my hands, twisting it to avoid twisting other things.

"If you hadn't been so busy getting your rocks off, maybe we could have gotten out of there in time."

"Getting my...I didn't hear you protesting."

"I was clearly out of my mind from...from trauma. You murdered a freaking dragon in front of me, not to mention three other people," she shouts, swinging an arm up to gesture around the room as if they're all still hanging around.

"I 'murdered' that dragon and those people because they were going to kill you," I shout right back, twisting around to lean closer to her.

Her eyes are dancing fire at me. "Yeah, because you brought me before Costecu like some prize. You put me in huge danger so you could save me? Is that it? Am I your damsel in distress?"

"What?" I splutter, not sure how to process what's going on.

"Why would you kidnap me in the first place, if we're supposed to be on the same side?" she exclaims, grabbing the duvet and pulling it up. I'm so angry and out of sorts I hadn't noticed it sliding down.

I shove the duvet off my lap and leap up, unable to sit still with this turmoil boiling inside. "Are you fucking kidding me? I had orders," I roar. "I had to maintain my cover. Costecu wanted you, and I couldn't compromise myself."

"There were other things you could've done."

"Like what? Rot in prison all my life? Come clean, ruin the operation, and lose my chance at revenge? He killed my family."

That stops her up short, but only for a second. "You could have told me. We could've worked something out."

I pace in front of her and the couch like a bull waiting for a red flag, flexing my hands open and closed. "I didn't know you. I couldn't trust you. I thought I'd either get you out like everyone else or sacrifice you to keep the mission going."

As soon as I say the words, I'm in trouble. I don't exactly wish I hadn't said them, because it was the truth at the time, but I wish I could have told her in a better time and place.

Her eyes slam open, and her chest flushes a bright red that doesn't reach her face. I'd be fascinated at discovering how far down the blush goes if she wasn't catapulting herself off the couch to shove both her finger and nose in my face to yell some more.

"You were going to *kill* me if it kept your petty goal of *revenge* alive?"

"Yes. Yes, I was. But then you had to go and be smart and clever and hot and extremely tenacious, and you pushed all my buttons and for some reason I really like you, and it doesn't make any sense, but then I had to save you, which I *did*, so you're fucking welcome."

I whirl around, needing to get out of here, far away. As far from this vexing creature who I can't seem to stop wanting to know every inch of even as she tortures me with stubbornness.

But then she grabs my wrist.

It would be trivial to pull away and storm off, but something inside me lets her tug me around. Maybe so I can shout some more, throw some curses and accusations, work out my anger against whatever ridiculous thing she's going to say next.

Instead, she jumps on me. I somehow have the presence of mind to catch her, but then all rational thought is burned away when she crushes her lips against mine.

Infuriating woman.

CHAPTER TWENTY-FOUR

Aideen

I've never been so angry with anyone in my entire life. One, he'd planned to literally throw me to the wolves if it got him the revenge he wanted. And two: he threw away all of the work I'd done to save my skin. It shouldn't be possible to be angry at someone for choices they've made that were in direct opposition to each other, but I'm managing it.

I don't know which is worse: the fact I'm so turned on by his admission he gave away everything to save my life, or the fact that it turns me on as much as it does. Worrying about my sanity can come later. I need to jump him.

So I do.

He catches me, secure as a baseball in a glove, and I grab the back of his head to crash my lips to his. I need his taste, his heat, and his strength, and I need it right fucking now.

The room spins, but it's not because I'm dizzy with lust, it's because he's spinning us, stumbling across the room like a top after too much wine. I'm deposited on my back on the couch with a bounce, where I have one second to drink in his chest and run my hands over hard muscles before he grabs me up again.

I don't complain, because it lets me kiss him again, which I do for as long as I'm allowed. His lips are strong, and he takes everything I give them, and when our teeth clack, he doesn't seem to mind, because he bites me. This twirling tour of the room is shorter and ends in the kitchen with my ass dropped onto the table.

I'd complain this is where I eat, except I don't, and I can buy a new table. Whatever he's got in mind is more important than a stupid hunk of wood. I move my hands to explore his shoulders, the muscles corded between his neck and his back, and I'm about to peel my mouth from his to bite their delicious firmness when he beats me to it.

His strong fingers grip the back of my head, tangling in my hair, and yank, exposing my neck to his frantic lips and teeth. Searing heat shoots across my skin as he finds my pulse and sucks hard. Then his hands are on my thighs, gripping tight, pushing them apart and pressing between them, and I'm so very ready. How long has it been? A week? It feels like it's been a week, but it can't have been more than a day or two. Still too long.

Bracing for the inevitable, it takes a second to register he's not pushing inside me like he should be. Instead, he's moving down, his lips trailing across the thin skin of my collarbone, making a detour to kiss and bite at my nipple.

I work my jaw in an attempt to protest, maybe, or complain about the lack of his penis doing penis things, but all I manage is some stuttering type of moan. It drives him to harder sucking, his hand behind my back holding me up as I fail to catch myself with my arms.

The cool air when his mouth leaves me is a shock, but I've got no time to process it because he nips down to my belly button, where his tongue swirls around in a lewd preview of what's to come.

"Ah...I'm not...not..." I'm not sure what I'm not. Not in my right mind. Not supposed to be this out of control. Not supposed to have sex with anyone before making sure they've been tested and going on at least four dates.

It's a bit late for that.

He growls against my skin, making it clear he doesn't care what I'm not. His mouth travels lower, and before he gets to the place of no return, he diverts and bites the inside of my thigh. I'm not a squealer, but the sudden sharp pain causes me to emit some sort of sound I've never heard before.

His hand leaves my back after sliding across my butt, and I have no choice but to drop back to the table, because the room is spinning for real now. I grab his hair and hold on tight, the darkest corners of my mind aware this is a ride I can't get off of.

I've never let anyone do this so soon. In fact, only one other man has, and it took months for me to build up the trust to let him. Yet here I am, mere days after having met Drew, and he's already got his face between my thighs, about to do something my imagination is already predicting to be the best and scariest thing ever.

I'm so wrapped up in fevered imaginations that when the tip of his tongue makes contact with my clit, it surprises me so much I squeak again. The next thing I notice is the roughness of his beard scratching my skin, and how gentle he's being.

Expecting something rough and fast, he surprises me by being gentle and slow. His tongue moves in small circles around my clit, which only serves to rev me up more. I hadn't realized how turned am I until I find myself speaking. "Don't fuck around. Please." It's more of a whine than a demand, and I might regret stooping to the depths of pleading later, but all I want is release.

He laughs, of all things, chuckling against my heat, the slight tremor of his jaw sending shivers down my legs. "Is there something you want, Zero?" he asks between slow licks up one side of my thigh and down the other.

"Fuck you." I drop a leg over his shoulder and shove my hips up into his face, but he moves back.

"Ah-ah, not yet. Not until—"

"Damn you. Just, aaah...just do it."

"So demanding," he chides, holding down one of my thighs with his large hand while he nibbles the soft skin around my throbbing lips, careful to stay away from anything that might trigger me.

"Bastard. You bastard," I gasp, working my hips, too far gone to be ashamed.

"They say honey, not vinegar, catches flies, Zero."

"Screw you."

"But I've always liked spicy more than sweet."

Thankfully I don't have to come up with a witty reply because his tongue does a thing that erases whatever garbage I was going to say.

There's no stopping what comes next, which is me. It's expected but still sudden, with no build up at all. The release is violent, crashing through my body like a living creature, consuming every ounce of energy that's been building since I woke up.

My eyes open once the room stops swimming. Somehow the ceiling is still there. I expected it to have been blown away by all the heat I'm pretty sure blasted out of mee.

"Geez, Zero. Save some for later," he laughs from somewhere down there. I'm no longer holding his head. My hands are flung out to my sides.

"Fmmghn," I manage to muster in protest.

"All right, come here." He rises like a leviathan from the deep, slides me off the edge of the table, and scoops me up into his strong arms. "Let's get you into bed. Damn it, wait, you have no bed. Why do you have no bed?"

I blink, slow as an owl. I can't stop focusing on his lips. "Why bed? I'm not sleepy."

"You sure? You look sleepy. Anyway, you don't have a bed. Why don't you have a bed?"

"This isn't my sleepy face," I say, reaching up to wrap hands around the back of his neck. Something is poking my butt. "This is my 'satisfied but wanting more' face."

"I'll remember that. But, again: no bed." He's walked us into the living room during this exchange.

"Doesn't matter. Not sleeping. Isn't this the point where you totally ravage me over and over, now that you've gotten the obligatory orgasm out of me?"

"You are one cynical person, Zero."

"Am I? I can feel your erection." I lock eyes with him, risking falling into them, but willing to take that chance.

"As if it's my fault you're super attractive and alluring and I want to ravage you over and over." The corners of his eyes wrinkle when he tries not to laugh.

"But you were going to put me to bed?"

"Zero." He assumes that faux-shocked look I've seen before. "Do you think so poorly of me still? Haven't I done my best to take care of you? I'd never ravage you when you're tired."

"What if I want you to?" I'm so comfortable in his arms I've stopped being worried about my feet being off the ground. Being suspended in the air has never felt so safe. If an earthquake struck right now, he wouldn't drop me.

"Zero, you don't have a bed."

"I thought you were more creative than that. Put me down."

"I kind of like you here."

"Put me down, you big lunk," I urge, pushing at his chest with both my hands. His pectorals are impressive in their solidness, no matter how many times I see them. The desire to keep looking and touching hasn't faded in the slightest.

"Zero..."

"If you think you should be 'taking care' of me, put me down right fucking now."

I watch his jaw muscles clench with satisfaction, and then he dips to set my feet on the floor, his hand sliding up my back until we're standing upright.

"Thank you," I say, and grab his length, wrapping fingers around heated hardness. "I can't suck you from up there."

"Zero—"

"Don't care what you're going to say." I drop to my knees and take a moment to examine him, for the first time, up close and personal.

If this were a fairytale, I'm sure he would be straight and smooth and perfect, but he isn't. A slight curve to the side and different skin tones give him character and make it real. That's about all the observations I care to make because I need to taste him. Not only that, I hope this will give him some motivation to figure out a workaround for the lack of a bed. I can conjure six possible options without breaking a sweat.

Breathless from the rush of this whole situation, the speed at which I went from angry to orgasm, I try to exercise some restraint. The salty tang teases my tongue as I take him in is strong, not my favorite taste, but that's not what matters. What matters is the stuttering groan he emits, a sign of his control slipping because of me.

As his hand lands on the back of my head and grips my hair, I get him as far as I can, then draw all the way off. My heart is doing flip-flops. I've never wanted to do this so much. It's more than wanting to make him feel good. It's I can bring this powerful man to those noises, and it makes me feel good, too.

"Zero," he says again, voice rasping against the air.

"I'll blow you until you come, if you want," I say, meaning it for once, laying a string of kisses along his length. "But I really, really...really...want to have sex again. And if you mention the lack of bed, I will bite it right off."

While he's above me, trying to stifle a groan, I take him in again, savoring the smooth slide against my tongue. Slow and rhythmic, getting used to the feel of him moving in my mouth, he might actually let me finish him off. Then he lets loose a guttural growl and hauls me up by my hair. The lightning shock in my scalp pulls me out of the meditative state I'd slipped into, and I grab at his wrist and shout.

"Ow, motherfucker."

The look on his face is a top five scary thing I've seen from him. It's as intense as the time he was facing off against the dragon, as concentrated as when he punched Costecu, and as fiery as when he stared me down through the window all those days ago, when this began.

He reaches out and grabs the couch, dragging it around in a half-arc toward us, the legs skipping against the hardwood floor, and before it's finished moving, he shoves me down over the arm. My ass is in the air, face planted onto the cushion, hands gripping at the duvet lying wrinkled on the couch where he'd left it. My mind might not have caught up yet, but my body knows what's coming next.

A hand lands on my hip, fingertips slide against my entrance, and then all the wind is knocked out of me as he slams inside. There's nothing I can do but clutch tight and hold on. It takes several seconds for me to catch my breath, during which he keeps driving into me, unrelenting. If I thought he was rough on me in the cabin, I was wrong.

My breaths come in short gasps, squeezed out of my lungs every time his hips meet my ass and his cock buries itself as deep as it can go in my pussy. Again and again he takes me, shoving a rough hand under my hips to move me where he wants, and I'm glad to give him everything.

A finger slides over my lips, finds my clit, and his fingers demand I come. There's no way I can resist. The second time is always better, and this is no exception. After the little warm-up on the kitchen table, everything is heightened.

For a split-second everything clenches, and I can feel every strong inch of him inside me before it all falls apart. My frantic pulses meet his needy pounding, and together we climax in the strongest joining I've ever had.

I come to my senses sometime later, with his lips on the back of my neck and his hands stroking my shoulders. The warm weight of him leaning over my back is more soothing than any duvet could ever be. I'm still bent over the arm of the couch, but I've never felt more comfortable in my entire life. Being dipped in warm honey couldn't come close to this.

"Okay, this is my sleepy face," I mumble.

He chuckles in my ear. "But Zero, you have no bed."

I pretend to struggle, kicking up at him with my feet. "I told you not to say that. Bring your dick over here so I can bite it off. I warned you."

"I'm willing to take that risk if it means your tongue on it again," he teases, tracing his lips over my ear.

"Horny perv. All you think about is sex."

"Very true. Since the minute I saw you all I've wanted to do is make love to you over and over."

"You call this making love? I might not be able to walk tomorrow." I don't bother hiding my smile.

"Then I'll carry you."

"You'll carry me to the office so I can make all the reports I need to make?"

He groans, stands up, and drags me with him, one hand sliding up my side to grab my breast. "Zero. That's the last thing you should be thinking about. I just screwed your brains out, and you're talking about work?"

I bite my lip to stuff down the grin. "We had adequate sex, very irresponsibly, after taking down a criminal organization. We should have gone right to the office to fill out paperwork."

His hand squeezes harder, his fingers tugging at my nipple, enough to make me squeak in pain.

"Zero," he growls. "Are you provoking me on purpose?"

"Now why on earth would I do that?" I ask, turning in his arms to bite his chin.

EPILOGUE

Druain

I'm awake before Zero, as usual. Ever since her promotion and our move to Seattle, life has gotten busier, but easier. She's in charge of more than one location these days. Bringing down Costecu brought her a lot of attention, and after the mandatory and frivolous disciplinary actions for what they called "reckless and dangerous" actions, she was promoted. However reckless they were, actions count.

They let me tag along, though I'm sure I was vilified even more for my actions. My guess, she put up a fuss, threatened to quit, and they caved. Every time I ask, she denies it, but I've seen the transcripts. It's the sweetest love letter I could imagine.

Officially, I'm her personal assistant with all the perks and salary that comes with being a PA for a high-ranking executive. I wear expensive suits to work, I go along with her whenever she travels, and I get to have sex with my boss. It's a dream job.

In a couple of days, we'll be flying to Memphis. I plan to eat a bunch of barbeque and stop her from working. This job lets me not only protect her from herself, but from the rest of the world. She has enemies, and not all of them are smart enough to stay away. No one will ever harm her while I draw breath.

My usual routine is to get up, get her coffee going, and then make two sunny-side-up eggs with bacon and oatmeal. Then the whole tray goes into the bedroom with me where I wake her up with a kiss and yank open the curtains.

Sometimes I simply tug her legs open. Morning sex is the best sex.

On the weekends things are a lot looser. If I let her, she'd stay in bed until noon, buried in blankets, hair splayed everywhere and her crabby gaze daring me to do something about it. Almost always, I have to drag her out from under the covers and into the shower, where she grumbles and punches me several times while I shampoo her hair. We tend to have sex afterwards.

We have a lot of sex. It's hard not to when almost everything she does is designed to provoke me into it. Or maybe it's the other way around. Either way, our chemistry hasn't faded. For the first few weeks after we put down Costecu, I was worried what we had might've been based on the dangerous situation we were in. But as life settled into normality, nothing changed. Actually, it got better.

I've learned her tenacity and stubbornness hide a vulnerable core. One I want to wrap up and protect with everything I've got so she can feel safe to be herself. Herself is a glorious and selfless person, one I can barely imagine I deserve.

I brush the hair out of her closed eyes as the thin sunshine starts to glow through the curtains. Seattle has been a great move for us. It's closer to the ocean she loves, and there're plenty of mountains and woods to go hiking in. My newest hobby.

I don't want to wake her. She's so peaceful when she's asleep. With the new job, she carries a fair amount of stress I have to work out of her every night. I try to keep her from working on weekends, though they're always trying to call her. Weekends mean work cell phones go in the safe.

I've got some plans for today. She's going to be pissed when I wake her up in two minutes at 7 am. I'm looking forward to the sound of her whine while she tries to keep the cover over her head. I'll try to find as many ways as possible to get it down. It's a fun game.

"Zero," I whisper in her ear, then kiss the shell.

She turns her head away, flinching, but doesn't wake up.

"Zero," I said again, licking her ear this time.

I'm rewarded with a grunt and more turning, but I've got my arm around her waist, and she can't get away. Her stomach clenches, one of the first tells I've learned means she's coming out of sleep. Having my hand splayed across her stomach every morning has its perks.

One of them is where I can go with it until I find what I want—so inviting, and impossible not to touch. I do, and then I bite her ear.

"Wrrgfnwhaauhnthe...uhn...hey..."

Her mumbling evolving into realization is another thing I adore about her so much. That moment of confusion when she's not sure where she is, but I've got her safe, and she knows I've got her safe. Or, at least, I've got her.

"Time to get up, Zero," I murmur as my finger plays inside her warmth.

"You're already up, you don't need me," she grumbles, smashing her face into the pillow, but the moisture on my finger tells another story.

"I'm up because it's so hard to stay asleep next to you."

"Cheesy bastard." Her voice is muffled.

"You know you like it."

"Not at fucking whatever morning shit time it is."

"Such a filthy mouth. I'm shocked. You taste so sweet."

"Oh my god," she groans. "Put it in and get it over with so I can go back to sleep."

A tempting offer, but not one I'm going to take her up on. Yet. I withdraw my finger now that she's awake. She tries to hide her sigh of disappointment, but I can sense it in the slope of her shoulders.

I rub those shoulders with my hand, my thumb stroking the skin between her shoulder blades, and I lean in to inhale the morning scent of her hair. "You're so beautiful."

"Don't think you can flatter your way out of waking me so early."

"Not trying to flatter my way out of anything. I'm the man, I can do whatever I want."

"Oh my fuck, why am I with you?"

"Because you love how strong and manly I am," I reply, turning her in my arms so she faces me. I want to kiss her, but if I did that, I wouldn't be able to look at her. The swoop of her nose, her proud cheekbones, every inch of soft skin that makes up Zero.

"Uh-huh," she says, unimpressed, but I know behind her skeptical eyes is the warm heart of the most amazing woman I've ever known.

"I want to put a baby in you." It's not the most elegant thing I've ever said, but it's slipped out already. As soon as I've said it, I realize I mean it.

She rolls her eyes and groans, while her leg slides and curls over mine. "You're the worst."

"Zero." Cradling her face in my hands, I hold her gaze. "I'm serious."

"What?" Her brows furrow, her expression registering confusion.

"Let's start a family. You and me."

She stares at me, unblinking, with that blankness I've learned is her processing face, so I push on before I lose my nerve.

"I know this is sudden, we haven't really talked about it, but every moment with you is paradise, and every second away from you is torture. I can't imagine spending my time or my life with anyone else. I want a family with you. Us together, a little one, a little dwarf-selkie, selkie-dwarf, dwarkie, whatever. I know I want you forever and ever and I'm ready to be happy because—"

Thank goodness she cuts me off because I'm babbling. My nerves running my words together. Spilling my guts in the scariest thing I've ever done.

"Okay."

I take a breath. "Okay?"

"Okay." Her hands slide up my back and come to rest behind my head. "I love you."

"I love you, too."

She leans and kisses a single tear off my cheek.

For one delicious moment I close my eyes, overwhelmed by the future and all the possibilities it holds. All of them are happy. With her it couldn't be any other way.

Then I grab her hips and pivot, dragging her up, rising out of the covers like a dolphin in the surf, her hair a beautiful arc of darkness trailing behind her.

"Hey. Asshole," she exclaims, grabbing at blankets to try to cover herself up.

I look at her, a goddess incarnate. A whole host of lewd things I want to do to her races through my mind. Luckily, we've got all the time in the world.

"Are you ready to get impregnated?"

"Holy shit. That's the worst line I've never heard."

She hits me in the chest, and I grin.

ABOUT THE AUTHOR

Cyprus Hart's earliest memory of trying to become a writer involves carrying a clipboard around and asking family members if the name "Rock Stone" was a good name for an action hero. Fast-forward three decades and he's still convinced he can make it work.

When he's not writing kissing, and other activities along those lines, into every book, he's tries to keep his border collie entertained and keep him and his chihuahua warm in the frozen tundra of Missouri.

Sorry – he doesn't like coffee *or* tea.

Connect with Cyprus:
website: www.cyprushart.com
IG: @AuthorCyprusHart
twitter: @CyprusHart

www.BOROUGHSPUBLISHINGGROUP.com

If you enjoyed this book, please write a review. Our authors appreciate the feedback, and it helps future readers find books they love. We welcome your comments and invite you to send them to info@boroughspublishinggroup.com.

Follow us on Facebook, Twitter and Instagram, and be sure to sign up for our newsletter for surprises and new releases from your favorite authors.

Are you an aspiring writer? Check out www.boroughspublishinggroup.com/submit and see if we can help you make your dreams come true.

Love podcasts? Enjoy ours at www.boroughspublishinggroup.com/podcast